1860

. . . Annie strained to catch the men's conversation through the dull rainfall. "Best to shoot it now and put it out of its misery," said the guard. A cry burst from Annie. Eyes swimming with hot tears, she rushed forward, breaking into the circle of men. "You can't shoot her, Pa!" she said urgently. "I don't know what's wrong with her, but you've got to give her a chance. . . ."

...FBEATS
OF DANGER

෴

by
Holly Hughes

Published by Pleasant Company Publications
© Copyright 1999 by Pleasant Company
For information, address: Book Editor, Pleasant Company Publications,
8400 Fairway Place, P.O. Box 620998, Middleton, WI 53562.

Printed in the United States of America.
99 00 01 02 03 04 05 06 RRD 10 9 8 7 6 5 4 3 2 1

History Mysteries™ and American Girl™
are trademarks of Pleasant Company.

PICTURE CREDITS

The following organizations have generously given permission to reprint illustrations contained in
"A Peek into the Past": p. 125—Wells Fargo Bank; pp. 126-127—Wells Fargo Bank (*Arrival of the
Pony Express* by A.O. Dinsdale; stagecoach print); pp. 128-129—St. Joseph Museum, St. Joseph, MO
(Pony Express ad); courtesy of the California History Room, California State Library, Sacramento,
CA (station); Buffalo Bill Historical Center, Cody, WY (mochila); U.S. Postal Service ("Wanted"
poster); *The Coming and Going of the Pony Express* by Frederic Remington, from the Collection of
Gilcrease Museum, Tulsa, acc. #0127.2333; pp. 130-131—Buffalo Bill Historical Center (Cody
photo); Wells Fargo Bank (envelopes); from a painting by George M. Ottinger, courtesy Library of
Congress (telegraph poles); Buffalo Bill Historical Center (posters).

Cover and Map Illustrations: Paul Bachem
Line Art: Greg Dearth
Editor: Peg Ross
Art Direction: Jane Varda
Design: Laura Moberly and Pat Tuchscherer

Library of Congress Cataloging-in-Publication Data

Hughes, Holly.
Hoofbeats of danger / by Holly Hughes.
p. cm. — (History mysteries ; 2)
"American girl."
Summary: In 1860, eleven-year-old Annie, who lives at the Red Buttes
Pony Express station in the Nebraska Territory, asks Pony Express rider Billy Cody
to help her find the person responsible for sabotaging her favorite pony Magpie.

ISBN 1-56247-814-1   ISBN 1-56247-758-7 (pbk.)
[1. Ponies—Fiction. 2. Pony express—Fiction. 3. Buffalo Bill, 1846-1917—Fiction.
4. Frontier and pioneer life—West (U.S.)—Fiction. 5. West (U.S.)—Fiction.
6. Mystery and detective stories.]
I. American girl (Middleton, Wis.) II. Title. III. Series.
PZ7.H87327Ho   1999   [Fic]—dc21   98-47807   CIP   AC

To Grace

Table of Contents

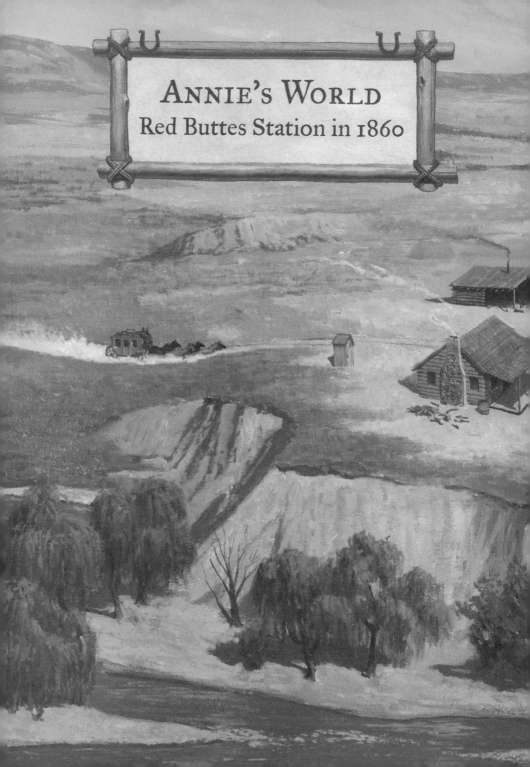

ANNIE'S WORLD
Red Buttes Station in 1860

CHAPTER I

THE MAIL MUST GO THROUGH

Lying on her back in the willow thicket, eleven-year-old Annie Dawson stared up at the clouds scudding eastward across the vast blue sky. Those same clouds came over the Continental Divide only a few hours ago, Annie thought to herself. They'll coast over the Great Plains next— maybe make it all the way east to the Mississippi River before they drop their rain.

Annie absentmindedly brushed her cheek with the tip of one of her long, silver-blond braids. She'd crossed the Mississippi River once herself, but she'd only been an infant then. She was born in the back of her parents' covered wagon, somewhere in Indiana on their way west from Vermont. That was in 1849, the year thousands of other fortune seekers had gone to California dreaming of gold.

"Someday I'll see what's east of the Mississippi," Annie murmured to herself. "Someday I'll ride a steam locomotive, or even a paddle wheel boat. I'll see the world, or my name ain't Annie Dawson."

Her thoughts were interrupted by a noisy woodpecker, drilling for bugs in the trunk of an alder tree. *Rat-tat-tat-tat-tat-tat.* Annie tipped her head back, hoping to catch a glimpse of his bright red crown. Nearby, autumn sunlight glinted on the bright leaves of a cottonwood, already shining gold for fall.

Just then, the trailing branches above her quivered and swayed. Annie held her breath. Was that the breeze, or had the ground trembled slightly? Listening, she thought she heard a low rumble, far away. "Davy, you hear that?"

Her six-year-old brother sat nearby, dreamily leafing through the worn McGuffey's Reader Annie had been using for his reading lessons. Dappled sunlight shone on his bowl-cut hair, straw-colored just like Annie's. "Hear what?" he asked.

"Hoofbeats," Annie declared, sitting up. She cocked her head to hear the faint sound echo off the mountain face. "It's the Pony Express rider, coming from the west." She scrambled to her feet. "That means it's Billy!"

Annie hiked up the skirt of her faded calico dress so she could run better. She dashed through the curtain of trailing willow branches and eyed the steep slope up from the river. Grabbing onto roots and tufts of hardy grass, she hauled herself rapidly up to the Red Buttes Station buildings on the rocky bluff above.

Annie hurried around the corner of the log station house, set on the highest vantage point of the bluff. A wide dirt yard sloped down from the station house to a low-slung log barn. A split-rail corral, empty at this time of day, stood to one side of the barn. A mass of pine scrub and sagebrush crowded up the eastern side of the bluff, as if the wilderness were hungry to reclaim this spot from civilization. But to the north and west, the bluff towered over a stark landscape of flat, rock-strewn plains. In the distance, three flat-topped buttes of rust-colored earth loomed above the land. It was these clay formations that had given Red Buttes Station its name.

The next Express rider, Tom Ward, came striding out of the station house. He had been waiting for several hours, knowing that the rider from the west was due any time. He shrugged his shoulders into a fringed buckskin jacket, holding a piece of fried cornbread between his teeth.

Annie's mother stood in the doorway behind him. "Won't do to leave without finishing your vittles, Tom," she said. "Not with a hard seventy-five-mile ride ahead of you."

Tom waved as he sprinted across the dirt yard to the barn. A moment later, he led out a tough little Appaloosa. Like many western horses, it had begun life in a herd of wild mustangs, then was caught by Indians and traded to white settlers, who'd broken it to the saddle.

The horse had been saddled up an hour ago, ready to set off whenever the relay rider arrived. The pony tossed his head, eager for a fast and furious run.

The hoofbeats were drumming closer now. Annie hurried to the spot where the hard-packed trail crested the bluff. Plucking a berry from a juniper bush, she gazed down the trail. The incoming horse and rider were hidden behind a cloud of dust.

Then Annie's heart leaped. There was Billy Cody all right, his wiry figure standing high in the stirrups. And underneath him was Annie's favorite pony, Magpie.

Annie danced impatiently from foot to foot. The black-and-white mustang lifted her head, spotting the girl, and surged up the bluff with one last burst of speed. Magpie galloped into the station yard, her hooves raising a cloud of dust.

Clinging to Magpie's neck, Billy Cody rolled out of the saddle. Before his boots had hit ground, he'd unhitched the mochila, a flat leather saddle cover with a mail pouch at each corner. Inside each of those four locked pockets were the precious letters to be delivered coast to coast in ten days by the new Pony Express mail service. To get this top-speed service, people paid top price—one dollar per half ounce of mail.

"Hey there, Tom!" Billy sent the mochila sailing through the air.

Tom grabbed it with one hand and swiftly slung it in

place over his own saddle. In a flash, he swung up on the Appaloosa. "See you next week, Billy!" He tugged quickly on the reins and tapped the pony with his spurs. The Appaloosa wheeled and took off toward the east, where the trail dipped into the pine scrub.

Billy grinned, his teeth shining white in the middle of his dust-grimed face. "A right quick handoff that time," he declared, sounding pleased. "And one of my fastest relays ever. Magpie done herself proud."

Annie skipped over to take Magpie's reins from Billy. Her sides still heaving, the mare whickered and nudged Annie with her soft pink muzzle. Annie laid her cheek against the pony's shoulder, feeling the mare's hot sweat sting her own skin. She could hear Magpie's heart hammering away inside her rib cage.

"It sure is good to see you again, girl," Annie said softly. It had been a week and a half since Magpie had galloped westward with another relay rider. A half dozen horses came in and out of Red Buttes regularly on Pony Express runs, but Annie yearned for the times when Magpie would be here, resting up for her next relay.

Magpie seemed to know it, too. She lifted her head expectantly. Annie, smiling, reached up to tug on the single white streak in Magpie's black mane, just behind her ears. Magpie closed her eyes as Annie scratched her black neck right at the base of the streak. Her long lashes—white on the left eye, black on the right—fluttered happily as she felt Annie's fingers rub her in that special place.

Billy Cody threw his lanky figure on the wooden bench outside the station house. He shoved his dusty hat back on his head, revealing a surprising band of clean forehead up near his sandy-colored hair. "I brought her home to you, Annie," he said with a playful smile. "Now don't you go spoiling her again. Magpie's a working girl—ain't you, Maggie?"

The mustang gave a little snort, for all the world as if she understood Billy's words. Annie and Billy laughed together.

Annie began to walk Magpie slowly around the station yard to cool her off after her hard run. "I'll groom her and feed her, Billy," she offered.

"That'd be right kind of you, Annie," Billy said. He stretched his arms wide and arched his back. Rising to his feet, he sauntered over to the water barrel near the station-house door. He took the tin scoop hanging beside it and filled it with cold well water. He drank thirstily, then took off his hat and poured a second scoop over his head.

With a satisfied sigh, Billy dropped back onto the bench. Davy, who'd wandered up from the river, came edging around the corner of the house. Billy winked at Davy, then set his hands on his knees.

"It weren't an easy ride, I can tell you," he began.

Annie and Davy traded delighted glances. They loved it when Billy launched into one of his tales. "I had to drag myself out of bed at Three Crossings before sunup. Ate my breakfast in the saddle—just hardtack and a hunk of cold salt pork. Didn't even get coffee. Then I ran into a flash flood—clean washed out a gully back in the Granite Range."

"How'd you get across, Billy?" Davy wondered.

"Talked the horse into jumping over," Billy replied. "He's a real whirlwind, a shaggy black gelding. You can't beat these mountain ponies for nerve. 'Course, I got stuck with an awful poky horse when I changed at Devil's Gate—lost some time there. Made up for it after Willow Springs when I got on Magpie. Lucky for me, 'cause when we hit the Rattlesnake Hills, we got set on by a pack of Indians."

Crooking an eyebrow, Annie turned to Billy. "Indians? Were they friendly?"

"I just said they set on me, didn't I?" Billy looked annoyed at her for spoiling the drama of his story. "It was a buffalo hunting party, braves armed to the teeth. Could've been Blackfeet."

Annie twisted her mouth skeptically. Magpie pawed at a few jagged rocks scattered at the edge of the yard, as if she too doubted Billy's word. "Those ain't Blackfoot lands, that far west," Annie said. "How were they dressed?" She knew as well as Billy did that there were several tribes in this vast Nebraska Territory, many of them peaceful. Why, just up the mountain lived a half-Shoshone girl named

Redbird Wilson. There were few young people around these deserted badlands, and the two girls had quickly become friends. Annie knew that Redbird's mother's people, the Shoshones, had always been friendly to white settlers.

"I bet they was Blackfeet. Blackfeet are the fiercest of all," Davy said. His face shone with admiration for Billy. "Weren't you scairt?"

"Naw, I'm never scared," Billy said, tousling Davy's fair hair. "But I sure enough felt a couple arrows whistle past my ears."

Annie halted in her tracks. "Oh, Billy! You didn't get hit, did you?"

Billy drew a deep sigh. "Had to ride like the wind, but I got away. I kept my scalp—this time."

Just then Mrs. Dawson stuck her head out of the station-house doorway. "Bill Cody," she said dryly, "is that you bragging out there?"

Billy gave Annie and Davy a guilty grimace and hopped to his feet. "Yes, ma'am."

Mrs. Dawson set her hands, rough from hard work, on her hips. She narrowed her hazel eyes. "Why, I can hardly recognize you for all the mud and dust," she scolded Billy lightly. "You give yourself a good scrubbing, hear? I took the liberty of washing your other shirt while you was away, but I won't let you have it 'til you're clean."

Billy made an exaggerated bow. "Yes, *ma'am*."

"Don't give me any of your sass now, boy," she replied.

"And you, Annie—soon as you've tended to that horse, haul me some water from the river." She turned and went back inside the dim, cool cabin.

"I better scoot down to the hay meadow and pick a nosegay for your ma," Billy said, nudging Annie with his elbow. "Don't want to be getting on her bad side. Mrs. Moore at Three Crossings don't do my laundry for me. Her cooking ain't near as good as your ma's, either."

Annie smiled, remembering what her mother had said just this morning. *I never can tell whether to treat that Billy Cody like a boy or a man,* she'd said. From her joshing tone, Annie could tell how much Mrs. Dawson liked Billy, in spite of all his mischief. A good thing, too, with Billy staying here every few days, waiting to ride the next relay back to Three Crossings.

Billy started to stroll down the trail he'd just ridden up. Annie knew he was heading for the meadow by the river, where the station's stablehand, Jeremiah, was harvesting the tall grass for hay. A ragged patch of wildflowers always grew at the edge of the meadow—sweet vetch, prairie-star, saxifrage, roseroot. Davy trailed behind Billy, idly whipping with a willow frond at the bushes beside the trail.

Annie turned her attention back to Magpie. Laying a hand on the mare's side, Annie could feel that her breathing and heartbeat had eased. She leaned against Magpie's powerful flanks, fitting the hollow of her temple against

the familiar place where the mare's hipbone curved out-
ward. Magpie shifted her weight to press gently against
Annie, too. Close up, Annie studied the way the black
hairs grew in round whorls on the mare's barrel.

Annie sighed and shook herself. She had to remember
that Magpie—like all the other horses in the Red Buttes
barn—belonged to the Overland Express company, not to
her. She'd better cover Magpie with a blanket before her
sweaty coat got cold. She clucked softly and turned the
horse's head toward the barn.

A trail of smoke rose from the chimney pipe of the
forge, a wooden shed set to one side of the barn. Back in
the California gold-mining camps, Annie's father had set
himself to learn the blacksmith's trade when he'd wearily
begun to give up his dreams of finding gold. That skill had
helped him get hired as a stationmaster almost a year ago.

Though few white settlers lived on these bleak plains,
this track was the main route west through the Rockies.
The North Platte River ran particularly shallow below this
rocky rise, and pioneers had long used it as a fording
place. A couple of years ago, the Overland Express company had taken over a meager trading post on the bluff
to serve various Overland enterprises. The Pony Express,
with twice-a-week relays in each direction, was the
Overland's newest service. Two weekly Overland stagecoaches also rumbled through the station—one eastbound,
one westbound. Mule-drawn wagon trains of freight rolled

in from time to time, too, and in the summer there were occasional wagons of settlers, bound for Oregon or California. There was always plenty of blacksmithing for Mr. Dawson.

Now Annie's father stood in the forge doorway, wiping his large, strong hands on a dirty cloth. He was a stocky, silent man with a dark beard. Annie could feel his eyes on her as she walked Magpie past.

"Annie!" he barked.

Annie jumped. What had she done wrong now?

Mr. Dawson stepped forward with a worried scowl. "What's wrong with that horse?" he demanded.

CHAPTER 2
WATCHING AND WORRYING

Annie froze. Something wrong with Magpie? "What do you mean—" she began.

Mr. Dawson's eyebrows met in one dark line. "Can't you see she's favoring her left hind foot?"

He strode quickly across the yard and picked up the mare's back leg, steadying her flank with his other hand. Magpie, taken by surprise, jerked her head up, then lowered it. Annie cradled the mare's trembling head against her chest. She ran her fingertips gently over Magpie's hard cheekbones, feeling the horse's muscles gradually uncoil, trusting human hands.

Mr. Dawson grunted. "Loose shoe." He set down Magpie's leg. "Who rode this horse in?"

"Bill Cody," Annie answered in a small voice.

Mr. Dawson shook his head. "I should have known. Where's he gone to?"

Annie's throat tightened. She gestured silently toward the hay meadow.

Her father set his jaw, his mouth disappearing in the bearlike beard. He strode toward the meadow, bellowing, "Cody!"

Annie hunched her shoulders, feeling somehow responsible for getting Billy in trouble. When things around the station went wrong, her father always seemed to overreact like this. She'd seen him be so gentle with animals; why didn't he realize that the same kind manner worked best with people, too? Miserably, she gathered Magpie's reins and led her inside the wooden barn.

The scent of hay and horses hung heavy in the dimness. Annie tethered Magpie beside the tack room, near the barn door. The surrounding stalls were full of the soothing sounds of horses munching, sighing, and stamping. But as she began to unsaddle Magpie, loud voices entering the station yard outside cut into the barn's calm.

"How can I believe you?" her father was saying angrily. "It ain't the first time you've been careless with the horses. Just last week you saddled Surefoot over a crumpled saddle blanket. He got a sore on his withers from it."

Billy's voice rose in protest. "But Magpie's hoof was fine, honest. She must have knocked it loose after—"

Mr. Dawson cut him off. "The Overland Express paid top dollar to buy the best horseflesh in the West. These little nags run their hearts out for the Overland Express.

How else could they get mail from St. Joe to Sacramento in ten days? You riders—you're just the weight in the saddle. You haven't got the right to mistreat the company's animals."

Annie felt tears spring to her eyes as she flung a coarse wool blanket over the mare's back. She knew exactly how Billy must be feeling. Just like Billy, she all too often did the wrong thing in front of her pa. She wanted so much to please him, but when he got that anxious look in his eyes, she immediately became tense, clumsy, and forgetful.

His stocky shape loomed suddenly in the barn doorway. Annie jumped, as if he'd read her thoughts. "You done with that horse?" he asked. Annie nodded. "Then bring her 'round to the forge."

As he began to step away, Annie cleared her throat. "Pa? You know, Magpie wasn't limping when she first arrived. I saw her run in and she was perfectly fine. But later she was pawing at some rocks in the yard—"

Mr. Dawson turned, still frowning. "Riders like Billy—they only want to be adventure heroes," he grumbled. "They ain't got responsibility to the Overland Express owners. But I do."

Annie almost blurted out "Pa, you're being unfair!"—but she bit the words back. It was useless to quarrel with her father when he was worried about station matters.

Pa lifted Magpie's hoof again. "Well, her hoof don't look injured," he admitted. "We'd best take precautions, though." He set down her hoof and took her halter. "Go to the remedy cabinet, Annie, and get some salve. Meet me in the forge."

As he led Magpie out of the barn, Annie slipped into the tack room, where a wooden cupboard hung in the corner. Inside were medicines for various horse ailments. Pushing aside a couple of bottles of belladonna and some muscle liniment, she found a small red tin of hoof salve. She took it and hurried back to the forge.

As she came around the corner of the barn, she saw her mother standing in the forge doorway. "I heard you light into Billy," she was saying to her husband. "What did he do?"

Slipping around her ma, Annie saw her father lower his head. "He misused a horse," he muttered as Annie gave him the salve. She realized with surprise that he seemed embarrassed about his outburst.

"Well, the animal's all right now," her mother said mildly. "Billy's just a boy, remember. He can be careless, but I don't reckon he meant any harm."

Mr. Dawson turned away, bending over the glowing coals of the forge's fire. He thrust a new horseshoe into the coals with a long-handled pair of tongs. Annie silently took Magpie's head, circling one arm around the mare's bowed neck. She lightly rubbed the special spot below the white streak in Magpie's mane. Her eyes fastened on her pa's strong hands, deftly handling the tools of his trade.

Pa carried the red-hot shoe over to his anvil to hammer it into shape. He hit it three times fiercely—*clang, clang, clang!* Then he hung his arm at his side. "This is no time to let things go slack, Effie," he said to Annie's mother, his voice thick with emotion. "Just when we've finally got things going right. This place has been good for us, for all of us. I can't let you down again. If I lose this job—"

"You ain't going to lose this job," Ma said with quiet conviction.

A darkness flickered over Pa's face—the same darkness Annie had seen when things went sour in California. He shook his head grimly. "The Overland Express is having money troubles—one of the coach drivers told me about it last week. The Butterfield company's trying to run us out of business. The Overland needs to win the government mail contract, but Butterfield and his cronies are fighting 'em in Congress. You know what happens when bosses start to get edgy. They crack down on the stationmasters—crack down hard."

Annie anxiously clutched Magpie's halter as her father bent to hammer on the new shoe. What if her pa lost this job? Annie had been sad to leave the mining camp in California, but now she'd hate to go back. There was food on the table every day now. They lived in a sturdy cabin, not a flimsy mining-town shack. She loved the wide blue sky, the rolling river, the fierce red clay and gray stone thrusting in strange shapes out of the earth. And she loved the excitement of living at the Overland station, with wagon trains and stagecoaches and Pony Express riders passing through. She felt proud, like she herself was the gatekeeper to the West.

Magpie raised her velvety muzzle, as if she sensed the worry settling in Annie's chest like a lump of lead. Annie scratched the mare's neck again, to soothe herself as much as Magpie. Then another thought stabbed Annie's heart. If Pa got fired by the Overland, she'd have to leave Magpie, too!

Mr. Dawson stood up. "Let's see how that fits." Annie silently led Magpie out of the smoky forge to circle around the sun-dappled station yard. The mare walked perfectly. Pa nodded, satisfied with his skilled work, and ducked back inside.

Whistling softly, Annie led Magpie back into the shadowy barn, going to her stall at the back of the barn. She stripped off the blanket, then took a clean rag to rub the mare dry. Using strong circular strokes, she ruffled Magpie's dense coat, feeling how much thicker it had grown in just a few days. "Putting on your winter coat already, aren't you, girl?" she murmured. Magpie whickered and gave her head a little toss.

Laying down the rag, Annie picked up a stiff-bristled brush. She pulled it expertly over the contours of the horse's back, eyes closed, her hands following every curve and hollow by heart. As she brushed, Annie felt her spirits rise. She opened her eyes and lovingly traced the white-on-black patches she knew like a map—the butterfly shape on her haunches, the mantle across her withers, the perfectly round splotch on the left side of her neck, the small white spots splattered along her forelegs.

Suddenly her fingertips grazed against the "XP" branded high on Magpie's hindquarters. She halted with a small sigh. That was the proud mark of a horse fine enough to be owned by the Pony Express—and a reminder that Magpie belonged to Annie in heart only.

From the stall, Annie heard a wagon rumble into the yard. She slipped out to see who it was. The station's stablehand, Jeremiah, stood with a pitchfork on the seat of a ramshackle wagon filled with sun-dried cut grass. "You finished harvesting the meadow?" Annie asked him.

Tall, square-jawed Jeremiah simply nodded. He didn't talk much, but his calm manner and horse sense had earned Annie's deep trust over the past months at Red Buttes. He was somewhere between thirty and forty years old, with a bald spot just beginning to show in his light brown hair.

Jeremiah lifted a forkful of fresh hay and laid it in her arms. "Let me guess—Magpie's here?" he asked, his gaze taking in her glowing face.

Annie grinned. "She sure is, Jeremiah!"

She scooted back to toss the hay in Magpie's manger. The mare snorted and gently butted her head against

Annie's shoulder before thrusting her muzzle into the sweet, fragrant grass. Annie buried her face in Magpie's mane. "Only the best for you, girl," she whispered.

CHAPTER 3
CRIES OF DISTRESS

Rain began to pound on the station-house roof as the Dawsons, Billy, and Jeremiah gathered for supper. They sat on stools and benches around a crudely built wooden table that filled the center of the main room. Firelight flickered in the big fireplace, where the iron stew kettle hung on a hook. A kerosene lamp dangled on a chain over the table, but it wasn't lit; Mrs. Dawson didn't like to waste oil when they had no company. The rafters and the rough timber walls at the end of the long room were dusky with shadows.

"Good thing we got the rest of the hay brought in this afternoon," Mr. Dawson said to Jeremiah. "This rain would have spoiled the whole lot." Jeremiah nodded silently in reply.

"The eastbound stage is late—I hope the trail ain't washed out," Mrs. Dawson said, worried.

"When they do get here, the driver may decide to stop

overnight," Mr. Dawson considered. "We could use the extra money. Annie and Davy, if there's women or children on the coach, you sleep out in the tack room—give paying passengers your beds."

Annie perked up, hoping she could slip into Magpie's stall to sleep. She'd secretly done it often. She loved snuggling on the straw, lulled by the mare's warm breathing nearby.

Just then, she heard slogging hoofbeats and creaking wheels outside. All the station folk scrambled to their feet and crowded toward the door.

Peering around Jeremiah's shoulder, Annie saw the stagecoach lumber into the station yard. Through the pelting rain, she could see that the coach jolted unevenly, tilting too low on one side.

The driver pulled his team of six horses to a stop. Jumping down from his high seat, he shook a stream of rain off his oilcloth cloak. "Got a loose wheel rim, Dawson," he shouted through the downpour. "Soon as I get these passengers out, I'll need you in the forge."

"Glad to help, Mr. Slocum," Annie's father called back. Then he turned, eyes bright, to murmur to Mrs. Dawson, "Nate Slocum—one of the Overland's most trusted drivers. A good man to impress."

The stagecoach guard had jumped down also. He held the coach door open and helped six passengers down the folding steps. Ducking their heads, they dashed into the station. Mrs. Dawson moved to take their wet coats. "Davy, light the lamp," she ordered briskly.

Jeremiah, Billy, and Mr. Dawson had gone outside to help the driver and guard unhitch the horses. Annie stepped toward the door, hoping to lend a hand in the barn. Mrs. Dawson looked up sharply. "Annie, I'll need you in here. You serve supper to our guests, you hear?"

With an exasperated flounce, Annie went to the wide brick hearth. She picked up a stack of wooden bowls and began to ladle out lamb-and-bean stew from the kettle hanging over the fire. On each bowl she set a slice of fried cornbread. Davy carried the bowls to the passengers now seated at the table.

The passengers huddled over their meal, eating hungrily. Annie had noticed that some groups of passengers were friendly with each other, joking merrily as they ate. Others—like this one—were silent, maybe even downright sour. Cooped up together day and night for three weeks as they rumbled across the continent, maybe they'd gotten on each other's nerves.

Billy sidled into the house, shaking rain off his jacket. He winked at Annie. She rolled her eyes. She knew that Billy should be in the barn; Express riders were expected to work around the station between relays. Still, she ladled out a bowl of stew for him.

Davy popped up beside the woodbox. "Want to play the memory game, Davy?" Billy asked in an undertone. Davy nodded eagerly and plopped onto the bench beside Billy.

"Look around the room, then," Billy instructed Davy. "Fix in your mind everything you can see. If you want to be an Indian scout like I do, you've got to be sharp-eyed."

Annie perched on the end of the bench, twirling the tip of one braid as she studied the room. She and Billy had played this game often, and Annie was good at it. She counted five coach passengers. There was a brown-haired woman in black, and her son—about eight years old, Annie guessed, with a chubby, spoiled face. Across the table from them sat two men with gray beards—one stout, with a red face, the other thin, pale, and wrinkled. "Red Fred and Dick the Stick," Billy whispered in Annie's ear. She smiled but nudged him to be quiet.

The fifth passenger, a thin man with glasses, held up his bowl. "May I have some more?" he asked in a reedy voice.

"Mr. Peeper," Billy whispered. Annie couldn't help but grin as she jumped up to serve the food.

The station door opened and the sixth passenger walked in, his head and shoulders soaked with rain. Annie guessed he'd gone to the outhouse. He was a young blond man with a yellow handlebar mustache. Raindrops dripped from its two absurdly curled ends. "Goldilocks," Billy whispered. Annie clapped a hand over her mouth to stifle a giggle.

Annie looked over at Davy. He'd slid down to the hearth and was staring into the fire, daydreaming. "So much for the memory game," she murmured to Billy.

"Some Indian scout *he'd* make."

"Aw, he's just a pup," Billy said. "No telling how he'll turn out when he grows up."

Annie sighed. "I don't reckon Davy will ever measure up for Pa. I mean, look how hard Pa is on me—he's so disappointed I'm a girl. It don't matter that I can hunt and ride and shoot—he wants a *boy* who can do all that. But that sure ain't Davy."

Billy set down his bowl with a clatter. "Well, I can do all those things, and your pa ain't a'tall fond of me. I reckon he's just hard to please."

Jeremiah and the guard came in from the barn, soon followed by Mr. Dawson and the coach driver, Mr. Slocum. Annie scurried to fetch their food. Jeremiah took a bowl of stew from her with a husky "Thanks" and tugged the end of one of her pale braids. Annie flashed him a little smile.

Then she handed a bowl to the coach guard, a heavy-set man in an olive green coat. He took it with a cheerful, hungry look. She didn't recall seeing him before. She remembered Mr. Slocum, though—a tall, silver-haired, rugged man with cold, hawklike blue eyes. "Best jehu on the Overland Trail," she'd heard her pa say, using the common nickname for coach drivers. "And don't he know it."

Nate Slocum stood eating by the front door, peering out into the rain. Then he turned to the room, wiping his mouth with the back of his hand. "Folks, we'll stay here overnight," he announced. "With this storm, it don't make sense to travel in the dark. And Mr. Dawson thinks it'll take him an hour or so to mend that wheel rim."

He glared at Pa, as if he thought the repair could be done faster. Annie threw a nervous glance at her father, remembering her parents' conversation earlier. Was Pa's job at stake?

Suddenly from the barn came frantic whinnying, and then a high, wild neigh. Annie froze, dropping the stew ladle. For a moment there was utter silence. Then a splintering crash split the night.

Jeremiah, Mr. Dawson, and Nate Slocum jumped to their feet. They ran out the station door, leaving it open behind them. Billy and the stagecoach guard hurried out after them, and the others crowded anxiously in the doorway. Seized with dread, Annie squirmed forward through the crowd. Unearthly as that animal cry had been, there was something familiar in it. . . .

Hoping against hope, Annie peered out into the wet darkness. Her heart lurched as she saw a black-and-white blur in the barn doorway. The world seemed to stop for an instant. It was Magpie, bucking grotesquely, hooves flailing, eyes rolling.

Annie clung to the rough doorpost, feeling sick and hollow. What was wrong with Magpie? It almost looked as if . . .

Had Magpie gone mad?

CHAPTER 4
AN EXTRA CHANCE

Fiercely Annie shoved past the coach passengers in the doorway. Mrs. Dawson reached out and grabbed her by the shoulder. "Let the men handle this," she muttered.

The scene in the yard was blurred by rain, but Annie could see Jeremiah trying to get a rope around Magpie's neck. As the men hemmed her in, Magpie wrenched away, pitching her body sideways. Annie spotted Billy by the horse's head, trying desperately to grab her halter.

Behind them, the coach guard dashed out of the barn, whip in hand. When Annie saw the whip, she lunged forward, a cry rising in her throat. Mrs. Dawson yanked her back, more firmly this time.

She heard someone in the crowd behind her say, "Give it a good lashing—that'd make the beast mind its manners." Annie spun around. The passenger that Billy had called Goldilocks was grinning to the bespectacled man beside him. He looked startled at the glare Annie gave him, and nervously twirled his mustache.

When she turned back, she saw a rope looped crazily around Magpie's neck, with Jeremiah tugging on its end. Annie bit her lip, watching the rope tauten and strain. The men began to close in on the horse again. Magpie made strange bleating whinnies. Annie shut her eyes tight.

"Should we wrestle her into the barn?" she heard Jeremiah's voice shout, almost lost in the drumming rain.

"No—the way she's kicking, she might crash through a wall," her father yelled back. "She could get hurt, and for sure she'd get the other horses all stirred up. Better put her out in the corral."

As she opened her eyes again, Annie saw the five men shoving and leaning against the frantic horse, forcing her into the corral next to the barn. Magpie, resisting, dug in with her hooves, splattering their faces with mud. But with all hands working, she was pushed inside the fence at last. Jeremiah dashed out after the other men, slamming the gate shut. The men headed back toward the house.

Relieved that the struggle was over, the onlookers moved with a murmur of conversation back to the table and hearth. Only Annie was left, clinging fearfully to the doorpost. Alone, she watched Magpie snort and make a few confused runs at the split-rail fence, as if aiming to jump it. Then she stopped, stiff-legged, wheezing, head hanging low. Annie saw a dreadful spasm twist the mare's body.

The white patch on her withers shuddered and twitched.

A few yards away, Annie could hear the Overland employees, huddling under the wide, overhanging eaves of the station house. She strained to catch their conversation through the dull rainfall. "She was fine when I changed her shoe this noontime," Mr. Dawson was protesting. "Gentle as always. My little girl held her head while I was shoeing her."

"These wild ponies—I've seen 'em go loco like this," she heard Jeremiah say in a glum voice. "They go back to being wild, being feared of humans. There ain't no cause, and there ain't no cure. It's a darn shame to see it happen to a fine horse like Magpie."

"Best to shoot it now and put it out of its misery," put in the guard. There was a rumble of agreement from the other men. "Want me to fetch my gun, Dawson?"

A cry burst from Annie, and the men halted, turning in surprise. Eyes swimming with hot tears, she rushed forward, breaking into the circle of men. "You can't shoot her, Pa!" she said urgently. "I don't know what's wrong with her, but you've got to give her a chance. Magpie's so sweet-tempered, she *wouldn't* turn against humans like that."

Her father looked at her, startled. Water dripped from his shaggy dark hair and beard. "Better stay out of this, Annie," he warned.

Annie dug her fingernails into her palms. "But Pa, I know that horse," she pleaded. "I've slept in her stall—

a few minutes, listening to the raspy snorts and whinnies coming from the corral. Those strangled noises didn't sound like Magpie—and yet it was as if Magpie were trying to tell her something. But what?

A faint light flared across the yard from the barn as Jeremiah and Billy settled into the hayloft for the night. Annie couldn't bear to go back into the house yet, but she couldn't stay outside in this downpour. Head down, she set off across the station yard to the barn, yanking her shoes out of the sucking mud at each step. Hurrying inside, she took a lantern from a hook by the tack room door. She lit it and headed down the aisle to Magpie's stall.

Pausing on the threshold, Annie stared into the silent stall, so strangely empty now. Her throat tightened, and suddenly she felt her chest heaving with sobs. She dropped to her knees, then threw herself face forward onto the straw-covered floor. Scalding tears brimmed over and ran down her cheeks.

If only Magpie could be here again, her old self! The thought spun round and round in Annie's mind, swelling into a stubborn hope. As she focused on that vision, Annie felt certainty surge within her. She just *knew* Magpie wasn't loco. There *had* to be another explanation. Magpie was sick or injured, and she needed help, not a bullet to the brain. None of the men understood that—only Annie did. "It's up to me, then," Annie said, lifting her head defiantly. "I'll save you, Magpie—I swear I will."

she's eaten her oats right out of my hand. A horse like that doesn't go wild again."

Billy raised his voice. "You're a good horseman, Mr. Dawson—you know what she's saying is true."

Pa flashed him a sharp glance.

"She must be sick or hurt." Annie pressed her point. "Why don't we send for Redbird Wilson? She knows a lot about healing animals. Remember the time we took her that goat with the broken leg?"

Her father hesitated, considering. They could hear a dull thud as Magpie flung herself against the side of the barn. "Well, I don't know," he said, his gaze flickering toward Nate Slocum. "I guess it's worth a try. After all, she's one of the fastest ponies the Express has got."

The stagecoach guard folded his thick arms. "Who's this Redbird Wilson you're talking about?" he asked curiously, cocking one eyebrow.

Mr. Dawson ran his fingers through his hair. "She's a girl who lives up the mountain just west of here. I reckon she's sixteen years old or so. Her pa's a mountain man, her ma's a Shoshone. The Shoshone grandpa is a healer. He's been teaching Redbird."

The guard looked shocked. "You'd let an Injun doctor that horse, Dawson? Why, you know the Injuns have been trying to shut down the Pony Express ever since it started. They attacked your rider this morning, didn't they?"

All eyes turned to Billy. He pulled back uneasily. "Well,

yeah, sure they set on me. But those were Blackfeet, not Shoshones. And they were just shooing me off their hunting ground—"

The coach guard clapped Nate Slocum on the shoulder. "You've been a jehu on this route for years, Nate. How many times you been attacked by Injuns?"

Nate Slocum frowned. "So often I've lost count."

The guard nodded and went on. "I haven't been working for the Overland long, but I do know the ways of the West. And one thing I can tell you is never trust an Injun. Blackfoot, Paiute, Apache, Sioux—they're all the same. They'll do anything to keep white men from settling the West."

Nate Slocum turned gravely to Mr. Dawson. "I'm of the same mind. Asking an Indian for help is just plumb foolish. I won't report this to headquarters, Dawson—but if I did, you'd get fired, sure as shooting."

The driver pushed past Annie and went inside to finish his supper. The guard followed close behind.

Annie, Billy, Pa, and Jeremiah faced each other under the dripping eaves. Annie fought to keep her voice from trembling as she said, "Pa, forget what they say. You know Redbird could help—she's got the healing touch. She nursed that billy goat for two weeks—"

"I ain't going against Nate Slocum, Annie," her father said firmly.

Annie raised her chin. "But he's wrong, Pa! Redbird wouldn't do us any harm."

Mr. Dawson shook his head. "I've got nothing ag[ainst] Redbird. But if anyone knows how the company bos[s] think, it's Nate Slocum. If he says they'd disapprove, taking the risk. Not with my job on the line."

"But if Magpie needs doctoring—" Annie began.

Her father cut her off. "Jeremiah's right—there ai[n't] doctoring for a horse that's turned loco. And a loco h[orse] is too dangerous to keep around. A bullet to the brain standard treatment." He studied her anguished face a[nd] sighed. "I'll grant you this much, Annie—I won't shoo[t] tonight." Annie's heart rose, and she flung her arms around her father. He awkwardly laid a hand on her ha[ir].

"But look here, Annie—don't get your hopes up," P[a] added uneasily. "If she's still acting crazy by daybreak, [I] got no choice but to shoot her. I won't let Nate Slocum report me for being slack." He turned away and, should[ers] hunched unhappily, walked back to his forge.

Annie watched him go. Billy tugged on her arm, urg[ing] her into the station house, but she shook her head. "I can't leave Magpie alone," she said in a choked voice.

Billy sighed. "You'll catch your death out here, Annie. Next thing you know, we'll be fetching Redbird to save *you*."

Annie hugged herself, feeling the chill of the raw, wet night. But she refused to give in. "I'll be all right," she declared hoarsely. "Just leave me be."

Billy shook his head and left with Jeremiah for the barn.

Annie stood alone under the station-house eaves for

Slowly she sat up, caught a long breath, and rubbed her eyes with her knuckles. *If I'm going to save her, I've got to think clearly,* Annie told herself. This stall was where Magpie's trouble began, she realized; maybe there was some clue here to explain what had happened to her. Lifting the lamp, Annie began to examine the straw scattered wildly on the stall floor. She imagined how Magpie's frantic pawing had tossed it around.

The mare's water bucket had been kicked over, too, splashing the wooden wall and leaving a pile of matted, wet straw. Annie groaned, sickened by the sudden thought that the feed or water she herself had fetched might have made Magpie ill. Steadying herself, she thought hard for a minute. She had gone all the way to the river to draw Magpie fresh water, rather than giving her the tepid water from the trough in the yard. But the river water couldn't have made her sick. Annie had also refilled the water barrel at the station house with river water, and none of the people drinking it had fallen ill.

Then what about Magpie's oats? Annie knew that eating spoiled oats could give a horse a serious, even fatal, case of colic. Warily she knelt down and fingered a few oats scattered on the stall floor. She laid one on her tongue, letting its papery taste dissolve. There was no bitter or moldy flavor, nothing to suggest that the oats had made Magpie ill.

Baffled, Annie gazed around the lamp-lit stall. She

noticed a few sharp, fresh gouges halfway up the wall, no doubt carved by Magpie's flying hooves. Annie felt her heart wrench as she imagined Magpie overwhelmed by pain or fear. *What was it, girl?* Annie's thoughts went out to Magpie. *What made you act this way?* If only she could find some clue.

Rain hammered on the roof, and the wind creaked the barn timbers. She could barely hear Magpie charging around the corral outside. But she knew the horse was still there, wet and cold, probably racked with pain. Annie wearily slipped to her feet and headed out into the rain again.

Pressing against the corral fence, her face lashed with cold raindrops, she whistled to Magpie. The mare gave one startled whinny and made a ragged dash, head down, toward the girl's figure. She veered aside at the last minute with a wild jerk. Snorting and wheezing, she danced away on stiff legs.

"Magpie! Maggie! It's me!" Annie called softly.

The mustang came to a wary halt. Trembling and shivering, she faced Annie. The whites showed dangerously around her eyes, but she held still.

Annie bunched up her sodden dress and climbed the rails of the fence. She hopped down on the other side, then edged forward, holding out a hand for the mare to sniff. Magpie quivered and snorted raggedly.

Getting closer, Annie reached for Magpie's halter. The

horse flinched and backed away a few inches as the girl's hand brushed her coat. Annie, murmuring gently, followed her. This time she got her hand on the cheek strap and took a firm grip.

Ribs heaving, legs trembling, Magpie stood rigidly still. Annie ran her fingers all along the halter. She felt no burr, no twisted bit of rope, nothing that could be irritating the horse. Hope fading, she dropped her hand. Magpie squealed and jerked away, fleeing to the far side of the corral.

Annie stubbornly followed, sloshing through the mud. Reaching Magpie's side again, Annie laid a careful hand on the mare's barrel. She felt her heart hammering inside, felt the ragged catch of her breathing. Then Magpie reared away, backing into the fence with a resounding crash of wood.

From the corner of her eye, Annie saw light stream out as the door of the station house opened. Then she heard a sound she knew well—the metallic snap of a rifle being cocked, ready to shoot.

Annie wheeled around. Through the slanting rain, she saw her father's silhouette in the open doorway, outlined in the yellow glow of lamplight. Her breath stopped. He was raising the long barrel of his rifle to his shoulder—and pointing it directly at Magpie.

CHAPTER 5
COURTING DANGER

"Pa, stop!" Annie cried urgently. Uncertainly, her father lowered his rifle. "Annie? What in tarnation are you doing in there? You want to get yourself killed?"

Annie slipped through the fence rails in a flash and raced across the yard. "Pa, I was only trying to calm her down," she pleaded.

Her father laid his rifle on his shoulder, but his face was grim. "Thank the Lord you're all right, child. I heard wood breaking—I feared she was busting out. If she's getting worse, I'll have to shoot her now, Annie, not wait for morning."

"She ain't, Pa," Annie said quickly.

Mr. Dawson took hold of her shoulder firmly. "Annie, I don't want you going near that horse again—you hear? You've got to stop thinking of her as the old Magpie. If she's loco, you don't want nothing to do with her."

"Why is everyone so all-fired certain she's gone loco?" Annie asked hotly.

"What else could it be, Annie?" Pa nodded toward the corral. They both turned to look at Magpie, pacing in circles in the rain, huffing and swinging her head wildly from side to side.

Annie tried to swallow the lump of dread that had lodged in her throat. "I've been trying to find what's wrong with her, Pa," she said, ducking under the eaves of the cabin. "I went out to take a look around her stall. I checked out her feed and water to see if something made her sick."

Her father studied her, surprised. "And what did you find?"

Annie dropped her head a little. "Well—nothing," she admitted. "But there *must* be some reason why she's acting like this." She paused, searching for the words that would reach her father best. "If she's sick, the company would want you to treat her, not kill her—wouldn't they? You said yourself she's one of the Overland's best horses."

Pa gave Annie a long look, as though noticing for the first time how grown-up she was. He stood silent for a moment, fingering his shaggy beard. Annie looked back at Magpie's restless shape through the blur of rain.

Her father's voice cut into her thoughts. "Nate Slocum's watching every move I make," he said. "That guard, too— he seems thick as thieves with Slocum. I'll bet anything they're under special orders from the company. I feel like they're just waiting for me to make a mistake."

Annie held her breath. Her father had never talked to her like this before.

"Why would they want *you* to get in trouble?" Annie asked, confused. "You're not their enemy—you work for the same company."

Mr. Dawson shook his head. "But I'm still new here. And I'm a failed prospector, not an innkeeper or trading-post owner like some of the stationmasters. The Overland took a chance by hiring me, you see, and I've still got to prove myself. If they don't think I'm right for this job . . . well, I've never felt Nate Slocum favored me," he confessed. "He makes me awful nervous, like he thinks I can't do nothing right."

Annie's eyes widened. Even her father, who seemed so strong and tough, felt scared inside sometimes. It had never occurred to her that someone like Nate Slocum could have the same effect on her pa that her pa had on *her*!

"And that new guard, Ambrose," Pa went on. "He seems a friendly sort, but he was sure asking me a lot of questions in the barn earlier. Wanted to know how we do this, where we keep that, all sorts of things. Every time I turn around, I feel his eyes on me, checking up on me—"

Just then, the guard's stout figure swung into the doorway. "Dawson?" he called out. "No point to standing around in the wet, my friend. I hope nothing's wrong?"

"I'm just on my way back to the forge—got to work on that wheel," Annie's father replied.

The guard shrugged. "Well, let me know if you need any help. I'll be happy to lend a hand." He moved back inside.

"You'd best go see if your ma has any work she needs done," Pa told Annie, patting her shoulder. "Take my gun back inside. There's a good girl." He handed her his rifle and then brushed past, hunching his shoulders as he waded back into the rain.

Annie watched him go with a wondering gaze. Now she understood why her pa often acted gruff. He had trusted her with his worries—and she was determined to live up to that trust. *There must be a way to help Pa protect his job,* she said to herself. Deep in her bones, she knew that saving Magpie—not shooting her—was the key.

Annie went unwillingly into the station house. How could she bear to stay inside, doing dumb chores, when she should be out searching for a way to help Magpie?

As she entered the house, she felt relieved, despite herself, to get out of the rain. She longed to go near the fireplace, but Nate Slocum and the guard were huddled in conversation by the hearth. She watched them uneasily from across the room, remembering her father's words. What were they talking about? Comparing notes on how the Dawsons ran the station?

The woman passenger rose to her feet. "If it's all right with you, Mrs. Dawson, I'll turn in now," she announced.

"Come along, Horace." Her son scrambled to his feet, greedily licking crumbs of cornbread from his fingers.

"Annie, show our guests to the other room," Ma said. Her quick gaze took in Annie's sodden dress. "And fetch something dry to change into. The barn will be none too warm tonight."

"Yes, ma'am," Annie said. She led the woman and her son through a doorway into the narrow, windowless room where the Dawsons slept. A big quilt-covered bed took up most of the space.

The woman gave the mattress an appraising pat. "Feather bed," she noted with approval. "Well, I surely intend to sleep well tonight. After fifteen straight days and nights in that stagecoach, my bones have been jolted and jounced as much as they can take."

Annie leaned down to pull out the trundle, a low bed that fit neatly under the bigger one. "Your son can sleep here in our bed." Horace wrinkled his nose as he fingered the worn patchwork coverlet on the trundle.

Turning on her heel, Annie silently grabbed her brown woolen dress from a shelf and moved behind a standing screen to change clothes. As she peeled the wet dress from her skin, she fought the impulse to make a rude remark to Horace. Her mother had told her time and again, always be nice to the coach passengers. They were paying guests, after all, and the Dawsons depended on the money they brought in.

Once her dress was changed, Annie hurried out of the
bedroom, doing her best to avoid talking with Horace and
his mother. Back in the main room, the other passengers
were getting ready to bed down too. Mrs. Dawson passed
out coarse wool blankets. A couple of the men passengers
pushed aside the plank table so that they could stretch out
on the bare, packed-dirt floor.

One of the older men was going out the front door,
headed for the outhouse, no doubt. "Take an oar with
you—you'll need it in this flood," called out the young
blond man with the mustache. "Say, Mr. Slocum, if we all
pitch together in the morning, maybe we can turn the
coach into an ark."

The driver looked up briefly from his conversation
with the guard. "Might be a good idea—it'd save Dawson
the trouble of fixing that wheel," he joked sourly.

Hearing his remark, Mrs. Dawson flicked an irritated
glance at Nate Slocum. She turned to Annie, handing her
two blankets. "Take a lantern when you and Davy go to
the barn. There's one by the door. You're sure you'll be all
right in there tonight?" A worry line creased Ma's forehead.

"The barn roof is plenty sound," Annie reminded her.
"And the straw will be warm. I'll wear Pa's woolen coat,
too. It's not as if I ain't slept there before—" Annie's voice
broke off. Before, she'd always slept with Magpie in her
stall. Tears welled up as she remembered afresh how
different it would be tonight.

Mrs. Dawson saw the tears in her daughter's eyes and immediately guessed the cause. She slid a consoling arm around Annie's shoulders. "I'm sorry Magpie's ailing, Annie. Maybe she'll be better in the morning. We can hope so, can't we?"

Annie nodded frantically, struggling not to sob. But her mother's kind words had opened floodgates inside her. She stumbled quickly to the door, hiding her face with the blankets. She didn't want anybody to see her crying and feel sorry for her.

Annie paused, staring at the plank door before her, willing her tears away. *It won't do Magpie any good for me to start blubbering,* she told herself. Daybreak was still hours away. She might yet be able to find out what had caused Magpie's illness—but not by dawdling inside the station house. Whatever was wrong with the horse, Annie felt sure there was one person who could help her figure it out—Redbird Wilson. But could she get Redbird's help in time?

Briskly she pulled a tin lantern off the narrow shelf by the door. It held a thick tallow candle, one of the batch she and her mother had made last week. She lit the candle's wick from a nearby oil lamp, fit the candle in place, then shut the small pierced-tin door of the lantern. "Davy?" she called to her brother, taking a worn jacket of lumpy black wool from a peg by the door.

Davy rose from the hearth, half-asleep and yawning.

Ma, banking the fire in the fireplace, turned to tousle his hair and wish him good night.

Annie stepped out the door, welcoming the chilly wet air. The rain seemed to have slackened, she noticed gratefully. Maybe a trip up the mountain was possible after all, she considered.

With Davy stumbling behind her like a sleepwalker, Annie led the way across the yard to the barn, holding their lantern high. As they slopped through the mud, she heard with a pang Magpie's fretful snorting and wheezing. She cast her eyes toward the corral and saw a dull gleam of white haunches in the murky night. Her whole body strained with yearning to go to Magpie. But she didn't dare go against her father's orders right now—it'd put him on his guard for sure. Glancing past the barn, she saw a red glow in the forge. Pa would be in there, working, for at least another hour.

As they entered the barn, Annie stepped over to pat Surefoot, a wiry roan stabled nearest the door. "You sleep in the tack room, Davy—I'll stay in Magpie's stall," Annie said, trying to sound casual.

"Magpie's stall?" Davy sounded confused. "But she ain't there."

Annie flinched at the thought, but she steeled herself to face it. "All the same, that's where I'm sleeping," she declared, stepping away from Surefoot and handing Davy his blanket. "You can keep the lantern."

Leaving a bewildered Davy in the tack room, she
marched in the dark to Magpie's stall. She felt her way in,
trying not to think about the heartbreaking stillness there.
She knelt to pat the straw into a bedlike heap. She heard a
faint sigh from the hayloft as one of the hands, Billy or
Jeremiah, turned over in his sleep.

She sat down, unlaced her stout brown shoes, and set
them by the stall door where she could find them later,
when it was time to slip outside. She tossed her father's
coat over the manger, then spread her blanket on the
straw. As she curled up on her makeshift bed, she saw the
gleam of Davy's lantern snuffed out. Silence settled over
the barn.

Annie lay rigid in the dark. If she fell asleep now, she
might not wake until morning—and that would ruin everything. She had to wait until everyone at the station was
asleep. No one must know where she was going. The very
idea of a girl her age going up the mountain alone in the
dead of night! Anyone who saw her would try to stop her.

Annie rubbed the tip of her braid anxiously against
her cheek. Time was running out; on foot, she'd never
make it up the mountain by dawn. The only answer was
to go on horseback. But on what horse? The Dawsons
had none of their own. When their old mule Jesse had
died in California, Pa couldn't afford to buy another. The
Overland had loaned them a team of oxen to haul their
wagonload of belongings to Red Buttes.

She held her breath, listening to the steady breathing of the horses in the stalls nearby, all of them the property of the Overland Express company. She'd ridden them all at one time or another, but only near the station, to exercise them between Express runs. To take one of them on a dangerous nighttime ride without permission—she knew it would be looked on as stealing.

But what other choice did she have?

Finally she heard her father closing up the forge; he must have finished repairing the stagecoach's wheel. She lay tensely, waiting until she heard the quiet thump of the station-house door closing behind him.

The wind had died down, and the rainfall had dwindled to a soft, steady patter. Beneath it all, Annie picked out the sound of the North Platte at the foot of the bluff. She was so used to that soothing, rushing noise that she barely noticed it anymore. But the river sounded louder than usual tonight—swollen by the rainstorm, Annie judged.

Shifting her weight cautiously, Annie sat up in the stillness. Her eyes, though accustomed now to the dark, could barely see the entrance of the stall. On her hands and knees, she groped over to her shoes and, fumbling, pulled them on. Then, feeling along the wall, she found the wool coat and shrugged it on.

Annie tiptoed to the tack room, fervently hoping Davy was asleep. After years of sharing the trundle bed with him, she recognized his ragged snores as she eased open the thin wooden door. She slipped inside, guessing from the snoring where Davy had spread his blanket. She surely didn't want to run the risk of stepping on him.

She knew the tack room's layout by heart, knew exactly where the bridle she needed was hung. Though Annie could easily ride a horse with just a halter, she'd feel better having a bridle for tonight's ride. Once she reached the upland trails, her life might depend on having the horse under firm control.

Edging along the rough wooden wall, she held one hand in front of her. In the blackness, she misjudged the distance and bumped into the next wall. She froze, listening tensely to make sure Davy hadn't awaked.

Reassured, she thrust out a hand again. Her fingers brushed against a pair of reins and she grasped them, the leather squeaking slightly under her touch. She lifted the bridle from its peg and slipped back out of the tack room, holding the metal bit to make sure it didn't jangle.

Stealthily, Annie headed for Surefoot's stall. She felt lucky that the wiry roan was at Red Buttes tonight, and in the stall nearest the barn door. Surefoot had earned his name for his skill at picking over difficult terrain. For the ride she had ahead of her, no horse could be better.

Surefoot, dozing on his feet, nickered in surprise as Annie entered his stall. But the pony knew Annie's scent and quieted at once. Her fingers felt clumsy as she slid his bridle over his head. She crooned to him softly to keep him calm.

Sliding her fingers inside the bridle's cheek strap, she led the horse toward the stall door. As Surefoot's hooves clopped softly on the straw-littered barn floor, Annie held her breath, praying that everyone at the station was asleep.

CHAPTER 6

THE MIDNIGHT RIDE

Annie froze, trembling. A dark figure blocked the barn doorway. She'd been caught!

"It's only me—Annie," she said in a small voice. "Who's there?"

"Annie, what are you doing?" The figure stepped out of the shadows. She saw, to her great relief, Billy's skinny figure, dressed in long red underwear.

Annie patted Surefoot's neck to steady him. She whispered, "I'm going up the mountain, Billy—to ask Redbird Wilson to help."

"At night? In this weather?" Billy whispered in alarm. "That mountain trail will be nothing but mud slides. You could break your neck—or Surefoot's."

Annie gripped the horse's reins. "I can't let Pa shoot Magpie. If I wait until morning, it'll be too late."

"Annie, I know how you feel. I couldn't sleep myself for worry over Magpie. But it's crazy to go out tonight."

Billy reached for Surefoot's bridle. "At least let me go instead."

"No, Billy," Annie said. Even she was surprised at the calm strength she felt now. "You'd lose your job if Pa caught you. Besides, you don't know the way." She led Surefoot past Billy and out into the station yard.

Billy followed. "You'll get your pa fired if Nate Slocum learns you've taken this horse without permission, Annie," he whispered urgently. "And Slocum flat out said you couldn't bring in an Indian healer."

Annie set her jaw. She'd reasoned through all this already. None of it mattered as much as saving Magpie. "He can't blame Pa if Pa doesn't know I'm doing it. And by the time Slocum finds out, Magpie will be cured. He won't complain then." She turned to go.

A fretful wheezing from the corral made both of them pause and listen unhappily. "I halfway think your pa suspects I did something to her," Billy muttered. "He was asking me all sorts of questions this evening. I felt so offended, I could hardly answer."

"Be patient with Pa," she replied softly. "He's afraid the Overland's fixing to fire him."

"Well, if someone's sabotaging the horses, it ain't me," Billy insisted.

Annie frowned as the meaning of Billy's words sank in. "Are you saying that someone *deliberately* hurt Magpie?"

Billy raised his eyebrows. "That horse wouldn't just go

loco, Annie. You and I both know that. Something else must have happened to her. Poison might've made her scream and kick and tremble like that."

"But who would do such an awful thing, Billy?"

He shrugged. "Who knows? Could be the Blackfeet, trying to stir up trouble. They'd do anything to drive us whites off their hunting grounds. Or what about the Butterfield Mail? They hate the fact that the Pony Express gets mail to California twice as fast as their service does."

Hearing an agitated whinny from Magpie, Annie drew in a sharp breath. "Well, right now all I know is that Magpie's suffering—and I've got to stop it. I'm going to fetch Redbird." She vaulted onto Surefoot's bare back. "You'll keep an eye on Magpie while I'm gone?"

"I promise. Good luck."

She rode Surefoot out of the yard, guiding him onto the grassy fringe where the sound of his hooves would be muffled. Once they had reached the trail heading west down the bluff, she gave him his head and urged him to pick up speed.

The rain had stopped falling, but a thick cover of clouds still hid the moon and stars. Annie tried to spot the buttes in the distance, but even they were obscured. She had to guess where the track lay by sensing where the grass stopped. She concentrated hard, relying on her memory of each curve and boulder that disrupted the westward trail.

The farther she got from the station, the less familiar the terrain became. She kept her ears tuned to the constant rumble of the river to her left, using the sound to guide her.

Though the wind had died down, the tall grass still swayed and hissed. Annie could hear small animals skittering about in the sagebrush—deer mice, gophers, jackrabbits. Surefoot shuddered with tension as he picked his way over the muddy, uneven ground. His legs jolted as his hooves struck unseen rocks.

As they pushed ahead through the darkness, Annie's thoughts turned back to her conversation with Billy. Could it be that someone had intentionally hurt Magpie? Annie hated the very idea, but she was running out of other explanations.

One thing Annie felt sure of—Magpie had been her old self when she'd galloped into the station yesterday. If anyone had poisoned her, it must have happened after Magpie was stabled in the barn. Annie considered Billy's remark that either the Blackfoot Indians or the Butterfield Mail folks might have a reason to sabotage an Overland Express horse. But Indians wouldn't have risked entering the station's barn only to poison a single horse. And no one from the Butterfield company was nearby—the Butterfield line crossed the country hundreds of miles to the south, through the old Spanish territories.

With a shiver of dread, she realized that it must have

been someone who was at the station that evening. Who'd had an opportunity to meddle with Magpie before she went loco?

Annie felt sure that none of the stagecoach passengers could have harmed Magpie. They'd all run straight from the coach into the station house, hadn't they? Then Annie stiffened, remembering the blond man—Goldilocks. He'd come in the house several minutes later. Where had he been? Maybe he'd only gone to the outhouse. But he could have slipped into the barn with no one seeing him, couldn't he?

Suddenly, Annie jolted wildly as Surefoot's left hind foot slid off the muddy trail and slipped toward the riverbank. Yanking her attention back to riding, she clung desperately with her knees as Surefoot made a sickening lurch toward the rushing river. Then the pony scrambled and caught his balance. She gasped with relief. She was lucky that neither she nor the horse had fallen.

Annie took a deep breath and urged Surefoot on. As he settled back into a steady trot, her thoughts returned to the early evening. *What about Nate Slocum?* a nagging voice inside her asked. He hadn't been in the station house at first—he'd been out in the barn, unhitching the horses. And so was that new guard. Jeremiah and her father had been there too, but they'd have been hard at work themselves. Could either the driver or the guard have approached Magpie unnoticed? Maybe.

Annie fidgeted, uneasily twisting the reins around her fingers. Was Nate Slocum beyond suspicion? He was one of the company's top drivers; surely he could be trusted. He might not like Mr. Dawson—might even hope to get him fired—but he wouldn't hurt one of the company's horses, would he? And if the guard was a company spy, as her father suspected, he'd hardly want to damage company property either.

All at once, Annie's thoughts were interrupted by a furious rustling right at her shoulder. Startled, she jerked on Surefoot's reins. With a fierce beating of wings, a marauding nighthawk flew past to land on a nearby bush. Annie saw its yellow eyes gleam through the darkness.

Annie looked around her with a creeping sense of dread. How long had she been riding? An hour? Two hours? With no moon to judge by, it was hard to tell how much time had passed. Halfway to the Wilsons', the route branched off on a side trail, winding up the steep face of Wilson's Mountain. Had she missed the pile of rocks that marked the turnoff?

She peered harder than ever at the low scrub on the right-hand side as Surefoot pressed on. A few paces farther, she spotted a pale gleam—the pyramid of white stones that Jake Wilson had set out years ago. Relieved, Annie pulled on Surefoot's reins, pointing his head up the rocky slope. The mustang snorted uneasily and balked. Annie slipped to the ground and went on foot, pulling the

horse behind her, remounting only when the slope became
more gradual.

The roar of the river soon faded away as pinewoods
closed in around them. The darkness of the plains seemed
nothing compared to the darkness of the woods. And
though the scraggly trees blocked the wind, the damp
mountain air made her feel the cold even more than she
had felt it in the valley. A shiver ran through her, and her
teeth began to chatter. A low-hanging pine bough, heavy
with raindrops, smacked her full in the face. Annie ducked
and raised one arm to ward off other branches as Surefoot
plodded forward. Annie told herself not to hurry him.
She had to trust the sturdy mountain pony. Magpie's life
depended on it.

Her mind flew back to Magpie. Who else might have
sabotaged her? Annie's heart sank as she realized she had
to consider each of the people who lived at the station—
her own family and Jeremiah and Billy.

She knew she could rule out Davy and her mother
straightaway. Davy was too young for such evil deeds, and
Mrs. Dawson had barely left the house all afternoon and
evening.

She refused to suspect her father, too, she thought,
pushing aside another drooping bough. He could be gruff,
but he wasn't cruel. And he stood to lose the most if anything happened to one of the horses in his care.

Jeremiah? He might be a quiet loner, but he was loyal

and honest—and he truly loved horses. That left only Billy Cody, she realized. But Billy, mischievous as he was, would never hurt Magpie—would he?

Annie rubbed her face wearily with one hand. She simply couldn't make sense of things. Maybe Redbird could help her figure it out.

Annie leaned forward to peer through the pine branches overhead. In the gaps, she spied the dark clouds breaking apart, rimmed with moonlight.

A few minutes later, the pony splashed across a shallow creek that Annie recognized. She felt a flush of triumph. The Wilsons' small, rough log cabin was only a few yards off, standing dark and silent among the gnarled pines.

Annie pulled Surefoot to a halt. Until now, she hadn't thought about how the Wilsons would react to her arrival in the dead of night. Her heart skipped a beat as she imagined Jake Wilson answering the door. She was more than a little afraid of the crusty, grizzled fur trapper, who'd lived off this bleak landscape for years.

CHAPTER 7

THE DARK BEFORE DAWN

Annie paused, listening nervously at the cabin door. She swallowed her fear and pounded a second time. Her muscles tightened, ready to dash away.

The door creaked open. Annie relaxed gratefully. It was Redbird, rubbing her eyes and looking confused. She clasped a shawl around her coarse linen night shift. Wisps of her raven black hair hung around her face. "Annie?" she said in amazement.

"I'm sorry to disturb you so late," Annie said in a rush. "But something terrible took place tonight." Quickly, she explained to her friend what had happened to Magpie. "They're planning to shoot her this morning," she finished. "Please, we've got to cure her before they get out their guns. I know you can do it, Redbird. If anything happens to her—" Annie's voice broke. Now that she'd finally found Redbird, all the fear and grief she'd been holding at bay came surging back.

Redbird put an arm around Annie. "I can't promise I'll be able to save Magpie, Annie," she said softly. "I have no idea what could be ailing her. But I'll try my best. Wait here a minute." She slipped back inside the cabin. Annie heard a sleepy murmur of voices inside. Waiting, she hugged her arms around herself, feeling the cold pierce her damp clothes now that she wasn't moving.

Redbird reappeared, pulling a buckskin dress over her shift. "I've got my pouch of remedies." She held up a small leather bag. "I'd best not take our horse—my pa might need it tomorrow. I'll ride behind you."

As Redbird pulled the cabin door shut, Annie asked, "Your ma didn't mind you coming out like this?"

Redbird shook her head. "My mother is the daughter of a healer. She knows we have to come when called, even in the middle of the night." The girl grimaced. "My father, on the other hand . . . well, I didn't wake him to tell him I was going."

Annie laughed ruefully as she swung up onto Surefoot. "I know. My pa's like that too."

With the moon out, the ride down the mountain went more quickly. Redbird sat behind Annie on Surefoot's back, her arms tight around Annie's waist. Their bodies warmed each other against the chilly night.

Redbird asked Annie many questions about Magpie's condition. Then she fell silent, mulling over the facts. "Reminds me of how horses act when they eat locoweed, but that plant doesn't grow much around here. It does sound like some kind of poisoning. If it wasn't something she ate by accident . . ."

Annie sighed. "I fed her myself. She got hay straight from our meadow, and her oats came from the same bin as all our other horses' oats." She paused as a thought struck her. "She did get a new horseshoe this afternoon. Could there have been something on the nails?" *The nails my own father drove into her hoof?* she added silently.

"I don't think so," Redbird replied. "The outside part of the hoof, where you drive the nails, has no veins in it— it's like our toenails and fingernails. A poison couldn't spread from there into the rest of her body."

Annie let out a breath of relief. She couldn't bear the thought that her father might be responsible. And she didn't like the idea that Magpie might have been poisoned in the afternoon, when the only people around the station had been people she knew well.

"Your father knows a good deal about horses. He may have some idea what caused this," Redbird went on. "When I speak with him—"

Annie felt uneasy. "Well, you see, Redbird, we can't rightly talk it over with him right now."

"Why not?" Redbird wondered.

Annie hesitated. How could she explain that she'd been forbidden to ask her friend's help—just because Redbird was an Indian?

But Redbird seemed to guess the truth, or at least part of it. "Ah, I see. So that's why *you* had to come for me," she said softly.

Annie looked over her shoulder, but Redbird's face was turned stiffly away. "I don't like it any better than you do, Redbird," she declared hotly. "And it ain't Pa who objects—it's the men from the Overland," she added, though she knew she wasn't exactly speaking the truth. "But they'll change their minds once you've cured Magpie."

"And what if I can't cure her?" Redbird asked.

Annie halted, not knowing how to reply to that. A silence fell between them, broken only by Surefoot's hoofbeats.

Finally Annie spoke up. "I'm the one asking you, Redbird—not them. No harm will come to you, I promise. I'll make sure of that, somehow. Even if you can't cure her, I'll be forever beholden to you for trying."

Redbird drew a breath, and Annie could feel her body soften again. "Maybe we can save her," she said, giving Annie's waist a reassuring squeeze. "It depends on many things—what kind of poison it was, how much she swallowed, how long ago it was given to her. . . . When you left, was she lying down, or was she moving around?"

"She was staggering around the corral, like she couldn't stand still," Annie said, shivering at the memory. "She broke out of her stall, and the men couldn't get her back in. I hated to think of her out in that rain all night—"

"But that's one thing in her favor," Redbird said. "She's got to keep moving, to help the poison work through her—and to prevent colic from setting in."

Annie's spine straightened with hope. "Then if we can just keep her walking around—"

Redbird nodded. "That would help, yes. It's the best thing we can do for her, if she's really been poisoned. But, Annie, there's no guarantee. Either the poison or colic could still mean the end for Magpie."

Annie felt her whole body go cold, even colder than it had been before.

Redbird seemed to read her thoughts. "The sooner we get to her, the better," she said.

"We have to get there before daybreak, anyway," Annie added, urging Surefoot on with her heels. "Pa said he'd have to shoot her if she wasn't better by then."

"I doubt she could recover that soon," Redbird warned. "It might take at least a full day—from sunset to sunset."

"Then if she ain't cured, we'll hide her from them," Annie decided. "Until the poison runs through her."

Redbird sighed. "Hiding a horse that's half-crazed with pain? How are we going to do that?"

"We'll find a way," Annie vowed.

By the time the girls neared the station house, the plains around them had begun to lighten with the coming day. The girls rode silently, both brooding over the task ahead.

At the foot of the station's bluff, Annie peered upward, hoping they could slip into the yard unseen. Her heart sank when she saw the stagecoach drawn up in front of the station-house door already. "Nate Slocum must be eager for an early start," she sighed.

She pulled Surefoot to a halt and slid to the ground. Redbird hopped off, too. Without a word between them, both girls understood that they had to approach the station with secrecy. They stepped off the track and, leading Surefoot by the reins, began to sneak through the grass, circling around to approach the station from the wooded side of the bluff.

"If we're careful, we might be able to sneak Surefoot into the barn," Annie whispered hopefully. "With the stagecoach team already harnessed, the men shouldn't be in the barn anymore."

As they silently rounded the back of the barn, Annie's eyes flew to the corral. Magpie stood huddled in a corner, swaying drunkenly on her feet. Her head hung low as if she were finally dozing. Her muscles were still twitching, her ribs still heaving. Annie's heart broke all over again. After her grueling ride, she'd half begun to feel her mission was over. But seeing Magpie again, she realized she still had a tough job ahead of her.

Moving quietly along the corral fence, she led Surefoot through the barn door and into the warmth and safety of his stall. Then she slipped outside to rejoin Redbird.

In the shadow of the barn, the girls crouched by the corral fence. "You stay here for a minute while I try to catch Magpie," Annie told Redbird. "I'm the only person she'll let near her. When you see I've got her, you get over to the gate and open it, quick and quiet as you can." She scooted between the fence rails and gave a low whistle.

The mare's eyes popped open and she whinnied shrilly. Annie froze, praying that no one would come round to investigate. Maybe they had grown used to Magpie's strange cries by now.

Magpie tossed her head and rolled her eyes. Spotting Annie in the lightening dawn, she recoiled slightly but stayed rooted to the spot. Swiftly, Annie came to her side. Her fingers sought out the white lock behind the mare's ears.

Magpie seemed to relax and lean into her gratefully. Still rubbing the special spot on the horse's neck, Annie took a firm grip on the halter with her other hand. She gave Magpie's head a gentle tug in the direction of the gate.

As soon as she felt her head being pulled, Magpie's eyes rolled back in terror. As she jerked her head backward, the worn rope halter came apart in Annie's hands. Annie quickly flung her arms around Magpie's neck and hung on like a burr.

Magpie shuddered wildly and began to buck. Annie buried her face in the black mane, clutching the white lock in her fist. She clung on desperately. Out of the corner of her eye, she saw Redbird waiting tensely right beside the gate.

Dimly, Annie was aware of footsteps pounding out of the barn. Twisting her head for a better look, she glimpsed the burly stagecoach guard, Mr. Ambrose, striding into the yard. In his right hand he waved something. Annie saw a metallic glint and guessed it was a long-barreled pistol. Redbird, frightened, dove between the fence rails into the corral.

With a sharp crack, the pistol fired into the air. Magpie neighed in terror and reared up, flinging Annie to the ground. Annie rolled away, cringing beneath the mare's hooves. She reached Redbird's side and the girls hugged each other for safety.

Now footsteps seemed to come from all parts of the station. A flurry of shouts arose.

Annie heard her father call out roughly to the guard, "What do you think you're doing, Ambrose?" The pistol fell to the ground with a sharp thud.

The guard answered urgently, "An Injun in the corral! Can't you see?"

As Magpie rocketed away from her, Annie dared to raise her head. She saw her father fumble with the latch of the corral gate, then swing the gate open. Magpie, head down like a bull, charged straight at him, making a reckless dash for freedom.

Pa tried desperately to get out of the horse's way, but

his right foot slid in the mud. Magpie reared, her forelegs pawing the air.

With a sickening *thunk,* her left forefoot caught Pa in the side of his head. He reeled backward, then fell limply to the ground.

Magpie wheeled and raced out of the open gate into the shadowy pine scrub.

CHAPTER 8

INTO THE WOODS

Annie didn't even remember running across the corral. The next thing she knew, she was kneeling beside her father. Her pulse pounded in her ears. All she could do was stare down at her father's motionless figure and the stain of dark blood on the ground beneath his head. Redbird knelt behind her, gently feeling Pa's wrist for his pulse.

Drawn by the uproar, people ran from all corners of the station—Billy, Jeremiah, Nate Slocum, various passengers. Mrs. Dawson came hurrying out of the station house, wiping her hands on her apron. As she reached the corral gate, all the color drained from her angular face. Pushing aside the onlookers, she knelt beside her husband.

"How did this happen?" she moaned, hoarse with emotion. No one replied at first, and her voice rose harshly. "Will someone please tell me what happened here?"

Ambrose bent over to pick up his gun. "That crazy

horse kicked him in the head," he said uncertainly. "It must have gotten spooked when I fired my gun."

"And why did you fire your gun?" Ma demanded, still not looking up. She reached out gingerly to touch the bloody gash in her husband's temple.

"I just fired a warning shot. I had to, when I saw that Injun near the corral." He nodded toward Redbird, who was kneeling just behind Annie.

Annie twisted her hands tensely in her lap, hearing the accusation behind his words. She saw her mother's eyes fly up, looking for an Indian intruder. But seeing Redbird instead, Ma closed her eyes gratefully. "Redbird! You're the answer to a prayer. We'll be needing your touch."

Nate Slocum strode past the knot of curious passengers. Annie saw genuine worry in his keen blue eyes as he looked at the stationmaster sprawled on the ground. "That's a nasty wound, Mrs. Dawson," the driver said. "Let's move him inside." He turned and motioned to three passengers standing behind him. "Give us a hand here, fellas. You there, take his feet." The skinny man in spectacles hastened to obey. The two gray-haired men eased their hands under Mr. Dawson's shoulders.

Nate Slocum gently cradled the stationmaster's injured head in his palms. "One, two, three, lift," Slocum said. The team hoisted Annie's father shoulder high and began to shuffle in step toward the station house. As Annie sprang out of their way, she noticed Davy and the boy named

Horace silhouetted in the firelit doorway, watching with frightened eyes. Seeing the men carrying the limp body toward him, Davy whimpered and scurried out of the way. Annie felt a stab of sympathy for her little brother, overlooked amid all the confusion.

As her father was carried inside, Annie stayed behind, feeling useless. She stared around the bare station yard, washed by the morning's first rays of thin sunlight. She saw Jeremiah and Billy standing by the fence, looking too shocked to tend to their chores. The stagecoach guard stood a little ways beyond them, his hands hanging at his sides.

Behind Annie, Redbird started to move silently toward the station house. Ambrose lunged forward and grabbed her by the shoulder. "You're the cause of this trouble. You stay right here," he declared.

Redbird froze.

Annie angrily thrust herself between the guard and her friend. "I brought Redbird here," she protested. "We were hoping to help Magpie. If that gunshot of yours hadn't scared her off—"

The guard tightened his grip on Redbird. "Are you sure she aimed to *help* that horse, Miss Dawson? You can't trust an Injun. They're all out to ruin the Pony Express."

Redbird stood still under his grasp, but her voice quivered with anger. "My mother's people have always been friendly to whites," she said with icy calm. "They welcomed my father into their village, even though he is a white man. Later my father helped build this very station house. We consider the Dawsons our neighbors—and our friends."

Ignoring Redbird, Ambrose turned to Annie. "Weren't you told yesterday not to bring this Injun down here? Don't you listen to your pa? This is a serious infraction of regulations. I hate to do this, but it's my duty to report it to headquarters. The Overland Express can't have station-masters who fraternize with Indians."

"Why not?" Annie snapped back.

The guard drew himself up to his full height. "Why, I've never heard such impertinence. A pretty little girl like you ought to have better manners. Seems clear we can't expect Dawson to run a station right. He can't even keep his family in line." He pursed his lips and shook his head regretfully. "This'll cost him his job, all right."

Annie defiantly crossed her arms, but she bit back her words. Why had she been so rash? she silently chided herself. It was more and more clear that this man was a spy for the Overland's bosses. Would her family have to leave Red Buttes now?

Just then Annie noticed that her mother had come up behind her. Ma shot Ambrose a dark look. "You're in no position to threaten others," she told him in a low, danger-ous voice. "You're the one who fired your gun recklessly. You caused a stationmaster to be injured, and allowed a valuable pony to escape. If anyone gets in trouble, it should be you."

She pushed his hand from Redbird's shoulder. "I know this girl; she's no threat to the station. In fact, we've always relied on the Wilsons for help. I need her help now in treating my husband. I'll thank you to let her go."

The guard frowned and shook his head, but he stepped away from Redbird. She turned and followed Mrs. Dawson into the station house. Annie wrapped a braid around one finger, uncertain whether to follow. If she went inside, would she just be in the way?

Ambrose stalked away, grumbling under his breath. Annie watched him go with a sinking feeling. He'd seemed genial before, but now she saw he had a vicious side as well. Annie feared that her mother's actions had only confirmed the spy's bad opinion of the Dawson family.

Ambrose headed for the stagecoach, which still stood in front of the door. The horses stamped their hooves and jingled their harness, waiting impatiently.

The blond man, the one Billy called Goldilocks, came around the corner of the cabin, a book tucked under his arm. He halted as he saw the coach waiting. "Ready to load up?" he asked the guard. "Or do I have time for another bowl of that excellent porridge?"

"You mean you haven't brought out your luggage yet?" Ambrose barked, looking up sharply at the passenger. "The rest was all strapped on a while ago. We'd be gone by now if there hadn't been all this fuss. You'd have been left behind, brother."

"Fuss? What fuss?" Goldilocks reached up to twirl his mustache. "I was just down by the river, below the bluff—I thought I'd get in a morning stroll while I had a chance. Sitting in a cramped coach all day and night is such a bore."

"Just get your luggage," the guard said with a disgusted wave of his hand. "We've got a schedule to keep." He turned away and busied himself with yanking tight the leather straps holding the pile of baggage atop the coach.

Annie watched the passenger saunter away, wondering if he was telling the truth. Maybe he really hadn't heard the shooting and the shouting. Standing below the rocky outcropping with the rain-swollen river thundering nearby, he might have been out of earshot. But it did seem odd. Why was this one passenger always absent when trouble broke out?

Billy came up behind Annie and muttered in her ear, "Goldilocks has been riding that stagecoach for two weeks. He's got to know better than to wander off when the stage is getting ready to leave."

Annie nodded. "I was thinking the same thing."

Billy frowned, tugging on one ear. "Funny things are going on here. Someone's up to no good."

The other passengers began to file out of the station house now, talking among themselves. Jeremiah slapped Billy on the shoulder as he passed, heading for the barn.

"See if you can find Magpie," he said. "Mr. Dawson and I agreed this morning, she has to be shot." He heaved a sigh. "If we'd done it sooner, he wouldn't be hurt now."

Annie saw an unwilling look cross Billy's face. "Aw, Jeremiah, she's already run away from the station—why don't we just let her go?"

Jeremiah shook his head. "She's dangerous, Billy. Besides, putting a bullet through her brain would be kinder than letting her break a leg out there and starve to death in some gulch." He glanced toward the loaded stagecoach. "We got to do things right. We can't let Slocum think we're careless."

Annie's head drooped. Jeremiah was right; they needed Mr. Slocum's good opinion to save her pa's job. But why did it have to be at the cost of Magpie's life? Then she threw a fearful look toward the station house. Would Pa be able to go on serving as stationmaster anyway?

Billy stopped at her side. "Sorry, Annie," he said gently as he began to load his revolver. "But maybe Jeremiah's right."

Annie clutched Billy's arm, the one that held the gun. "But Billy, she ain't loco!" she protested. "She was just spooked by that gunshot, that's why she kicked Pa." She lowered her voice. "Redbird reckons you were right about poison, Billy. She says Magpie needs to keep moving until the bad stuff runs through her. If you just say you couldn't find her—let her run loose until she's better—"

Billy looked uneasy. "You heard what Jeremiah said. In her condition, she could break a leg or even break her neck."

Annie tightened her fingers on his arm. "Then go find her and stay with her. Keep her safe. I just know she'll get better if we give her time."

Billy stared into her searching eyes. "What if she runs from me? You come with me. She won't run away if she sees you."

Annie dropped her eyes, shaking her head. "I can't leave—not with Pa lying in there like that."

"Redbird and your ma can doctor him just fine," Billy insisted. "We're no use to him in there. But if someone's poisoning Express ponies here, we have to stop it, for the sake of the Overland. That'd be more help to your pa than anything."

Annie straightened her shoulders. What Billy said made sense. This might be the chance she longed for to prove herself to her father. "Let's go, then," she decided.

With the passengers milling around the stagecoach, wondering when they might pull out, nobody noticed the boy and girl hurrying to the barn door. Billy quickly fetched a rope from a hook, and then the two headed for the pine scrub behind the barn. Billy gestured toward a gap in the foliage. Judging from the broken boughs and trampled sagebrush, it was a good guess that this was the way Magpie had run—away from the river, toward the open plains.

Billy started down the muddy slope into the scrubby woods. Annie hitched up her brown wool skirt to follow him, wishing as she often did that her mother would let her wear pants. Billy had little trouble scrambling down the slope in his riding boots with the pointed toes. Annie did the best she could in her stiff, thick-soled shoes.

Though the sun was rising ahead of them in the eastern sky, the dense scrub was still dark, the low overhead branches matted and heavy with last night's rain. Following the trail Magpie had thrashed through the wet pine scrub, Annie called out to Billy, "How can we ever catch her on foot? You know what a speedy little horse she is."

"The brush and trees will slow her down," Billy pointed out as he swung around a thorn bush. "And I'm betting she ain't running her usual pace. You saw how confused and worn out she was. Anyway, we've got to try." He sprinted ahead.

For ten minutes or so, Annie picked her way along, straining her ears for the sound of hoofbeats. Then she saw Billy halt ahead of her. She hurried to his side. He was staring down into a jagged gully.

Annie followed his gaze. There at the bottom of the gully, near the flooded creek, lay Magpie, her legs splayed awkwardly to one side. All around her sprawled a dense thicket of gray-green bushes, climbing halfway up the gully wall.

Holding onto a pine sapling, Annie lowered herself

into the gully. To her left, a fresh vertical gash, gouged deeply into the gully wall, suggested that Magpie had come down the same way—and probably by accident. *Please don't let her have a broken leg,* Annie prayed silently.

She threw an anxious glance at Magpie, not far below her. The pony seemed to have landed in the densest part of the thicket. For a moment, Annie felt relieved. The mass of tough branches would have cushioned the mare's fall. Annie charged toward Magpie. But as she reached the edge of the thicket, her skirt tore on a barrier of sharp thorns. "Sticker bushes!" she yelled to Billy, who was dropping down the gully wall behind her. "A whole big patch of 'em!"

As she waded in, the thorns bit cruelly into her skin. Even worse, they hooked the tough branches to each other like a huge springy net. Magpie must have flailed about and tangled herself even further, Annie realized.

Peering ahead to find a gap in the thorns, she saw Magpie shudder in agony as a spasm went through her. Coldness gripped Annie's heart.

Magpie was trapped in the brambles. She couldn't move.

Then how was she going to work the poison out of her body?

CHAPTER 9
TRAPPED!

Annie tore her skirt free and then stepped downward hard, trampling the brambles under her thick soles. Though the thorns dug into her ankles and stung her legs, she waded across the briar patch to Magpie. Nearing the horse's side, Annie held out her hand. But just then, another spasm took hold. Magpie flattened her ears and jerked her head around, trying to bite at her belly. Annie drew back, frightened. Her own stomach doubled up as she watched the pains rack Magpie's gut.

Billy halted at the edge of the briar patch. "Look at the way her stomach's heaving—like something's eating her up inside," Annie groaned. "And her breathing is so harsh. That's a sure sign she's sick, not crazy." Billy nodded grimly.

"We can't leave her lying still like this," Annie pressed on anxiously. "Have you got your knife with you?"

"Always," Billy replied. From his belt he pulled his long

hunting knife with the mother-of-pearl handle. Annie
knew it was one of his few prized possessions. He'd told
her it had been a gift from the great Indian scout Kit
Carson, though she suspected that was just another of his
tall tales.

Billy leaned over and began to saw at the thickest
bramble branches, hewing a path toward the trapped horse.
His silver blade flashed as he cut, and Magpie, eyeing him,
snorted nervously. "Hush now, girl," Annie crooned as she
began to yank aside snarled branches at her end. The mare
quivered but lay still.

Annie and Billy worked swiftly, urgently, both aware
of the desperate need to free Magpie so she could move
again. Feeling thorns slashing her palms, Annie dug her
hands into her skirt and doubled up the rough wool to
protect herself as she worked.

Finally Annie ripped away the last brambles snaring
Magpie's neck and shoulders. Without waiting for them
to clear any more away, Magpie heaved herself forward,
scrambling to her feet and through the narrow clearing
Billy had hacked open. Her hindquarters were scored with
bloody scratches.

Annie hurried after her, whistling for the mare to wait.
Magpie pricked her ears and jerked to a stop. Billy scooped
up the rope he'd brought and tossed it to Annie to slip
around Magpie's neck. As Annie leaned toward her, Magpie
shuddered with a fresh convulsion of pain and staggered a

few steps away. "It'll be all right, girl. It'll be all right,"
Annie said, trying to calm the anguished horse. She sidled
carefully toward her and got the rope around her neck.

Billy approached cautiously as Annie knotted the rope.
He thrust out an arm and pointed at Magpie's flank, his
face creased with concern. "There it is! Look on her rump,
Annie."

Annie peered carefully. Amid the fresh scratches from
the thorns she saw a deeper cut about three inches long,
its blood already dried, in the middle of the white patch
on Magpie's hindquarters. "What's that?" she asked, her
voice tightening.

"Your pa told me he saw it early this morning—I guess
Magpie was dozing, and he was able to sneak up and look
her over. He said he'd found an arrow wound on her flank."

"An arrow wound?" Annie wondered. "How can that
be? There wasn't a single mark on her coat when I groomed
her yesterday afternoon. I'd've noticed."

Billy nodded. "Your pa figured she got it yesterday,
when those Blackfeet attacked me."

Annie's shoulders sagged. "You mean . . . he thought
the Indians made Magpie sick? Tipped their arrows with
poison or something?"

Billy sighed. "Something along those lines. 'Course, I
insisted she hadn't been hit. But he didn't believe me. He
thought I just hadn't noticed the wound." He hung his
head. "You know, Annie, those braves didn't really shoot

any arrows at me at all. They just shouted from afar. I guess I exaggerated when I told the story later. I was just making up a brag—trying to look like a hero."

Annie frowned. "Your stories are always right entertaining, Billy," she said, "but it looks like this one's backfired. It could even lead to bloodshed."

Suddenly they both noticed that Magpie was standing still and swaying dizzily. Annie gave a gentle tug to the rope around the mare's neck. Magpie grunted and skittered a few steps, and then Annie began to pace her up and down along the creek bank, leading her by the rope. Magpie followed, trembling and wheezing roughly.

Keeping a watchful eye on her, Annie considered what they knew about Magpie's wound. "All right, we know for certain Magpie wasn't shot by an Indian arrow yesterday afternoon. But how do you explain this wound on her flank now? She was inside the barn from the time I finished grooming her to the time she started acting up."

"She was out in the corral during the night," Billy pointed out. "But it ain't likely any Blackfeet crept up in the night and shot her then. Not in a rainstorm, with a dozen people staying at the station."

"Even if they did, it wasn't the thing that made her go loco," Annie reminded him. "She was already acting crazy by then."

Annie watched another spasm grip the weary mustang, her own body shuddering in sympathy.

"I didn't have a chance to check out the wound this morning before she ran off," Billy said. He cautiously came closer to Magpie and peered at the wound. Then he gave Annie a grim look. "That's no arrow wound, Annie. Look at it yourself."

Annie held out her open hand until Magpie nuzzled it, her hot breath warming Annie's palm. Then Annie gently ran her hand along Magpie's side, moving cautiously to her sore flank. She delicately fingered the wound. Magpie flinched from her touch.

"It isn't deep enough for an arrow wound," Billy pointed out, "and the edges are too clean. They were cut with something sharper—a knife, maybe."

Annie saw that Billy was right. "But why? Who would take a knife to a horse like that?"

"It had to have happened in the barn yesterday, sometime after you groomed her," Billy said somberly. "But before she went crazy—nobody could have got near her then. That means it must have been somebody from the stagecoach. Or somebody from the station, Annie."

Before Annie could reply, Magpie made a strangled wheeze as another spasm shook her. Annie swallowed hard. Suddenly she felt overwhelmed. "Oh, Billy, what if she gets worse? What if . . . what if she dies?" Her eyes welled with tears and her mouth began to tremble.

Billy reached over to give Annie's shoulder a squeeze. "As long as she's got strength enough to keep walking, she's got a chance. And as long as we can keep her here, away from folks who'd like to shoot her—"

The image of her father crumpling to the ground flashed into Annie's mind. She shut her eyes tightly.

Billy sighed and went on. "My guess is that somebody planned that cut to look like an arrow wound. Maybe he overheard me last night bragging about being attacked— that could have planted the idea in his brain."

Annie pressed a weary hand to her forehead. "But why? What purpose would it serve?"

Billy shrugged. "It would sure enough make the Indians look bad. Maybe it's someone who hates Indians. Or somebody who's bent on stirring up trouble between the Indians and the Overland." He snapped his fingers. "That's it. Remember when the Paiute attacks shut down the Pony Express this summer? If the company thinks the Indians are interfering again, we could have a whole heap of trouble break out."

Just then Annie heard a rustle at the top of the ravine, and she ducked low. All this talk about sabotage and attacks was making her jumpy.

Glancing up, Annie saw Redbird peering down at them from the bank above. "Annie?" she called down. "Is everything all right?"

Hearing a new voice, Magpie shied and bolted a few yards down the gully, nearly pulling the rope out of Annie's hands. As Redbird joined Billy and Annie, Magpie shivered and lowered her head to drink thirstily at the creek. "We found Magpie all tangled up in the bramble patch," Annie told her friend. "Billy and I cut her loose."

"We're doing everything we can to keep her moving around," Billy added.

"How's Pa?" Annie asked Redbird anxiously. "He must be better or you wouldn't have left him, I know."

"He's resting easy now," Redbird said, "but he's still blacked out. We won't really know how bad he got hurt until he wakes up. Your mother's with him."

"Looks like Magpie's having terrible stomach cramps," Billy put in. "And look there." He pointed to the wound on Magpie's flank. "Someone cut her with a knife."

Redbird pulled out her remedy pouch, which was hanging on a leather thong around her neck. "I've got a little pot of salve in here that's good for flesh wounds. It'll help heal all those scratches from the sticker bushes, too."

She inched forward, approaching the fretful horse. Magpie watched with an uneasy eye, but stood still, as if she sensed Redbird could be trusted.

"Does it look like someone rubbed poison into that wound?" Annie asked as Redbird deftly worked the ointment into the pony's twitching flank.

"I just can't say for certain," Redbird said. "I hate to think anybody would do such a thing."

"I hate it, too," Annie declared, "but it's looking more and more likely. And what if other horses are hurt next?"

She rubbed her dirty hands on her skirt. "My pa's job is on the line already—we don't need anything more to go wrong. I can't just sit here. I'm going back to the station to see what I can find out."

"What about Magpie?" Redbird asked. "I can't stay here with her—I have to get back to your pa."

"You two go back. I'll stay," Billy offered.

"But Jeremiah expects your help in the barn," Annie reminded him. "You'll get in trouble if you're gone from the station much longer."

Billy dismissed that with a wave of his hand. "It's more important to me to take care of Magpie. I'm bound to get fired from this job soon, anyway. I'm not much of a company man."

Annie paused, looking at Billy for a moment in a new light. Suddenly she realized that Billy's days with the Pony Express were numbered. He'd come to be such a part of her life, she'd never imagined him moving on. But he was bound to—and sooner rather than later. She reached over and squeezed his wrist. "I'm beholden to you, Billy."

He looked away, embarrassed. "You just go back, girl. You won't figure out what's been going on as long as you're jabbering away here."

The two girls set off, hopping back over the creek. Redbird hoisted herself up the gully wall, then reached down to give Annie a hand.

They hurried back the way they had come. As they

jogged through the pine scrub, early morning light broke through the clouds. Birds sang as if glad the storm was over; Annie picked out the loose trill of a junco, the coo of a mourning dove, and the distinctive mew of a catbird. Sunbeams sparkled on the rain-drenched pine needles. The air was crisp and cool.

They were still some distance from the station when Annie heard the far-off crack of a whip and an ominous rumble of iron wheels. Startled, she jumped up on a granite boulder to look.

The stagecoach was jolting down the eastward track, leaving Red Buttes Station.

She urgently waved at Redbird. "They're going! Whoever poisoned Magpie could be riding away on that stage right now. We've got to stop them!"

Redbird scrambled up behind Annie on the rock. "Forget it, Annie," Redbird said, her eyes on the departing stage. "You'd never convince that driver to stop. You have no proof that anybody on that stagecoach did anything wrong."

Chapter 10

Hard Proof

Adread silence hung over the station as the girls entered the empty yard. Things often seemed extra quiet after a stage had left, Annie had noticed. But it was even worse today.

Without speaking, they went inside the station house. The main room was in disarray, with empty porridge bowls, tin mugs, and dirty spoons still sitting on the plank table. Annie set a tipped-over rocking chair back upright. Someone must have knocked it over when the sound of Pa's accident had first drawn everyone to the yard. In the distress ever since, no one had thought to right it again.

Redbird gave Annie a quick hug. "I'll be by his bedside if you need me," she said softly. "Good luck—I hope you can figure out who poisoned Magpie." She headed into the Dawsons' sleeping room.

Annie hung back, peering hesitantly through the half-open door. She could see her father's still form under the tattered quilt, and her mother seated on a wooden stool, her lips moving as she read the Bible.

Annie turned her face away. She'd seen her share of illness and death; disease had often raged through the poor, makeshift homes of the California mining camp. But she was still stunned to see her own father struck down. He had always seemed so strong, so hard, so tough.

"Annie?" came a small voice by the fireplace. Surprised, Annie noticed Davy, seated forlornly on the woodbox.

Her heart went out to her little brother. The best thing she could do for him was to keep matters as normal as possible, she figured. She took a deep breath, suddenly feeling bone weary from grief and strain—not to mention spending all last night riding in the rain. But the time to rest had not yet come.

"Heavens, who let that fire go out?" Annie asked briskly, "Have we got any kindling, Davy?"

Davy unfolded his tightly curled limbs. "Th-there's kindling here in the woodbox."

"Well, pile some on, and maybe add a couple new logs," Annie directed him. "I'll get the tinderbox to light the fire. Let's get this mess cleaned up before Ma comes out."

For once, Davy seemed glad to be told what to do. He and Annie bustled around the room, making up the fire and then clearing the table. She yearned to head out to the barn, to try to solve the riddle of what had happened to Magpie. But for the moment, Magpie was safe—

nobody was going to shoot her right now. And Annie was badly needed here.

Once the fire was blazing, Annie heated water in an iron kettle over the flames. She dipped each bowl in the kettle, scraped off the dried porridge with a stiff little bundle of straw, swirled the bowl around, and then handed it to Davy to dry.

"Annie?" Davy frowned at the bowl he was wiping dry. "How long do you figure it'll be before Pa gets better?"

"I don't rightly know," Annie answered. "But say, wasn't it lucky that Redbird was here already? Can you imagine if we'd had to ride up and fetch her *after* the accident? But instead she's right by his side, fixing him up as good as new."

Davy thrust out his chin doggedly. "Jeremiah said that was a powerful hard kick Magpie gave Pa," he said. "At first I was afraid she'd killed him. He still could die, couldn't he, Annie? Don't lie to me."

Annie paused, brought up short. She realized she'd been talking down to Davy. Her brother deserved more respect; he wasn't a baby anymore. "I reckon that's true, Davy," she admitted quietly. "I'm awful scared about him dying. You are too, aren't you? But all we can do is hope and pray."

Davy's blue eyes filled with tears. "I just wish I hadn't thought so many mean thoughts toward Pa," he mumbled. "I wish I could take them all back, right now!"

"I feel just the same way, Davy," Annie confessed with

a catch in her throat. She opened her arms and wrapped them around her little brother. They sat huddled like that for a few minutes.

Finally Annie let him go with a deep, comforted sigh. Jumping to her feet, she seized on a new task, folding the blankets that the coach passengers had left in a heap by the woodbox. Davy picked up a broom propped against the wall near the fireplace. He began to whistle as he swept the hearth.

Underneath the blankets Annie found the McGuffey's Reader Davy had been thumbing through yesterday. She slipped it into her pocket. Books were few and precious out here. With no school around, she was bound and determined to teach Davy his letters herself. She couldn't let him lose this book.

Carrying the pile of blankets to the chest of drawers, Annie forced herself to think about Magpie. She knew if she didn't, she'd begin to worry about her family's future—and right now, that was even more worrisome. Instead, she ran over yesterday's events once more in her mind. Who had had a chance to cut Magpie? Jeremiah and her pa, she remembered, had been going back and forth between the hay meadow and the barn all afternoon. Billy might have helped with the haying too, though Annie suspected he'd slipped off to the hayloft instead for an afternoon nap—he'd been dead tired after his hard ride. Once the stage-coach came in, however . . .

Suddenly, Annie noticed small thunking noises coming from the far corner of the room. "Davy? What are you doing?" She glanced over at her brother.

Davy was kneeling by the woodbox, the broom on the floor beside him. In his right hand he held a folding pocketknife. He cocked his wrist, then threw the knife at the log cabin wall. Its silver point pierced the wood and the knife stuck there, quivering.

Annie frowned. "Where'd you get that fancy knife, Davy?" she asked. "I've never seen it before. I'd remember something newfangled like that." Most of the men at the station, like Billy, carried long Indian-style knives in their belts, not clever folding contraptions like this.

Davy yanked the knife out of the wall and clutched it to his chest. "I found it out in the barn. I reckon one of the coach passengers dropped it. But they're gone now, Annie—I can keep it, can't I?" he pleaded. "Finders keepers, you know."

"When did you find it?" Annie asked, suspicion dawning. She shut the blanket chest and stepped over to get a closer look.

"Last night, after supper," Davy confessed slowly. "I guess I should've said something then, so the owner could claim it. But it's so fine, Annie!"

Annie took the knife from Davy. She turned it over in her hand curiously.

The knife had a dull brown handle and a short steel

blade. At the base of the blade, where it folded into the handle, was a flaking crust of something dark red.

"Where in the barn was it lying, Davy?" Annie asked sharply.

"On the floor—just outside Magpie's stall," Davy answered.

Annie pushed the blade backward on its spring. Twisted in the tiny hinge were a couple of horse hairs—white and black.

Here was the proof Annie needed. Someone *did* cut Magpie deliberately—using this very knife!

CHAPTER 11
SCENE OF THE CRIME

Annie held the telltale knife tight. "Can I take this, Davy?"

His face crumpled. "But it's mine, Annie—I found it first!"

"You can keep it for good, Davy, I promise. But I've got to have it for a little while just now. You see, this might tell us what happened to Magpie. I think someone used it to cut her. And maybe this will even help Pa."

"You mean that it will make his head stop hurting?" Davy looked puzzled.

Annie sighed. "Maybe not that. But it'll get him out of trouble with the Overland Express bosses. Oh, I don't have time to explain now, Davy. I have to look around the barn and see what else I can find."

Davy looked excited. "I'll finish tidying up for you," he offered. "I'll fill the woodbox and haul some water, too. And I'll feed the chickens—Ma hasn't done it yet today."

Annie was surprised. Maybe Davy wasn't lost in his daydreams as much as she'd thought. "I'm proud of you, Davy," she said, giving his shoulder a grateful pat. "Ma will be grateful too, I know she will. I'll go to the barn, then."

"Good luck," Davy called after her as she hurried out the door.

Annie dashed across the station yard to the barn, a flutter of hope in her chest. She wasn't sure what she was looking for, exactly. But if the poisoner had been distracted enough to drop his knife, maybe he'd left some other proof of his crime.

In the dim, hay-scented coolness, the horses were contentedly munching, stamping, and whisking their tails. Annie paused to listen for a second, relieved that no other ponies seemed to be sick. The poisoner must have gone after only one horse. *But why did it have to be Magpie?* she wondered, angrily kicking a stall doorpost with her shoe.

Then, as she walked down the row of stalls, she realized why Magpie had been chosen. It was simply because her stall was at the back of the barn, where the poisoner was most likely to escape notice.

Annie stopped at the entrance to Magpie's empty stall. She drew a deep breath to steady herself. Now that it was daylight, maybe she could see things she hadn't seen last night. The blanket she'd slept on still lay crumpled on the straw, she noted. That was good—it meant that Jeremiah hadn't yet come in to clean the stall. If anything suspicious was lying around, it hadn't been cleaned up.

Tossing her braids behind her shoulders, Annie knelt down and began carefully to look over the floor of the stall. Brushing the straw aside, she ran her fingers over every inch of the dirt floor, from the stall door to the back wall.

Near the back, she ran across a patch of mud under the littered straw. Annie's heartbeat began to speed up. This must tell her something! She turned to check where the overturned water bucket lay, but it was on the far side of the stall. It couldn't have made things muddy over here, she reasoned. Looking directly up, she saw sunlight streaming in through the stall window, halfway up the log wall. It was tightly shut now, with an iron latch, and she was sure it had been closed when she slept here last night. But the mud was pretty fresh, and there was a good deal of it. That window must have been open last night during the storm.

She sat back on her heels to think things through. Could the poisoner have climbed in that way, to avoid being seen by the men in the barn? Suddenly, with a chill, she remembered Goldilocks coming into the station house on his own. His clothes had been plenty wet. Could he have crept out to the barn and climbed through the stall window?

She stood up and looked more closely at the window itself. Though it was small, it was certainly big enough for a grown man to climb through.

Think logically, Annie told herself. All right. She knew the storm had started before the stagecoach arrived; she remembered hearing rain pound on the station-house roof as her family gathered for dinner. And Jeremiah hadn't gone out to the barn until *after* the stagecoach arrived, she recalled. Even if he'd closed the windows then, this patch of mud would already have been here.

Looking down at the floor again, Annie noticed something she hadn't seen before—an impression in the soft mud. Tense with excitement, she bent down to study it.

It was a footprint—a single footprint.

"What are you looking at, Annie?" Davy's voice broke into her thoughts. Startled, Annie whirled around to see her little brother in the stall doorway, eyes shining with curiosity. "Did you find some clues?" he asked.

Annie nodded. "Someone's left boot landed here in the mud last night," she explained, pointing to the footprint. She bent down and studied the print closely. "It ain't very deep. If someone had climbed in through that window, he'd have landed with a real thump. I reckon this was left by someone who just walked into the stall."

Davy squinted, as if trying to picture the intruder entering the stall. "The toe is pointing toward the back wall," he commented. "Someone climbing through the window would have landed the other way around."

Annie raised her eyebrows, impressed. "Good, Davy. Now, let's try to imagine just how things happened. This person must have been in the stall after the rain started, and before I came here to sleep. But nobody needed to enter Magpie's stall in all that time. The men tending to the coach horses had no call to be down at this end of the barn. And I'd already fed, groomed, and watered Magpie hours earlier."

Davy frowned. "Could that be *your* footprint? You were poking around the barn last evening—I noticed you had straw on your skirt when you came back into the house."

Surprised again at how much Davy had noticed, Annie paused. "That's true. But look here." She set her shoe next to the print. "This was made by a foot much larger than mine. Looks big enough to be a grown man's foot."

"So whose could it be?" Davy wondered.

"Well, let's think. Not Billy's—the toes on Billy's boots are more pointy than this, and Billy's boots have a high heel, to hold better in the stirrups."

"Pa's boots are all cracked and broken on the bottom," Davy recalled. "I always hear Ma telling him he's got to get some new ones, now that we have a little money saved up."

Annie nodded, grateful for Davy's help. "But I have no idea what Jeremiah's boots look like. Not to mention Nate Slocum's, or any of the coach passengers'." Frustrated, she bent down and, with a fierce intent, studied the print once more. "Look, Davy, see that pattern on the sole? All those zigzag ridges cut across the ball of the foot? The mud's preserved it, clear as day."

Davy leaned over to look. "There can't be too many boots with that design," he agreed.

Annie sat back on her heels with satisfaction. "I can compare this print to Jeremiah's boots. Maybe he stepped in the mud when he was shutting the window against the rain last night. Fair enough. But if this boot print is someone else's, it's a good guess that that someone was up to no good!"

Davy looked troubled. "But the stagecoach has already left, Annie," he said. "How could you compare this print to the boots Mr. Slocum wears, or the guard, or any of the passengers? You can't take this patch of mud anywhere."

Disappointed, Annie dropped her hands to her lap. She felt the McGuffey's Reader in her skirt pocket. A thought struck her, and she pulled the book out triumphantly. "Here's the answer, Davy! This blank page inside the front cover—there's room here to copy that boot print. I'll just need something to draw with. . . ."

"Pa's pen and inkwell, by his ledger in the tack room!" Davy declared. "I'll go get it." He dashed out of the stall.

As she jumped to her feet, Annie's mind danced. She could see it all now—the mystery man crowding into the stall with Magpie, treading on that muddy spot, ducking away from the rain leaking in. "Maybe Magpie bumped him up against this wall—" she said to herself.

Her eyes flew to the rough log wall. She froze.

Right in front of her, she spied a tuft of colored thread

on a splintered spot on the back wall. It looked to her as if someone had snagged his clothes on the wood.

Hardly daring to believe her luck, Annie leaned over and pulled a few threads from the wall. "Better leave some in place, just to prove this was where I found 'em," she muttered.

In the light that streamed through the cloudy window glass, she saw the color of the threads—a dull olive green. She rubbed them between her fingertips, feeling their rough texture. Wool, she guessed.

Now, who was wearing green wool last night? She shut her eyes to check her mental picture of everyone at the station. Jeremiah and her pa had been wearing brown. Mr. Slocum, she remembered, had on a mustard-colored oilcloth cloak. She squinted as she tried to recall Goldilocks' clothes. He'd been wearing a dark blue coat, she was pretty certain.

Then her heart skipped. The stagecoach guard! She saw him now in her mind's eye, sitting last night by the fireside, murmuring to Nate Slocum—wearing an olive green coat.

CHAPTER 12

IN THE NAME OF REVENGE

 nnie opened her eyes and shivered with excitement. "It's *got* to be him—the signs all point toward him!" she sang under her breath. "He was in the barn at the right time and everything!"

Then she halted suddenly. She remembered her pa's opinion that the guard was a company spy. It just didn't make sense that a fellow like that—a trusted insider—would want to injure an Overland Express horse.

Her thoughts were shattered by a commotion outside. Annie stood on her tiptoes to look out the window. Rumbling into the yard was a long string of heavy, mule-drawn wagons.

She heard Davy run back into the stall behind her. "I didn't know we were expecting a train of freight wagons today," she said over her shoulder.

"They must be running ahead of schedule," Davy suggested.

Annie turned back from the window. "I'd better go on out," she said, straightening up with a newfound sense of responsibility. "Pa's ill and Billy's off in the woods—Jeremiah'll need another hand to help the drovers feed and water those mules. And Ma can't cook for them today, not with Pa the way he is. But if they want to buy food, we could sure use the extra money."

Davy reached up to take the McGuffey's Reader from her. "You go on—I can copy the boot print."

Annie hesitated. She remembered the beautiful drawings Davy made on his slate sometimes when he was supposed to be doing sums. "I reckon you can, Davy," she said. "And we'll need it for sure, because I have an idea who may have poisoned Magpie. If that boot print matches his . . . well, you draw it as perfect as you can! I'll be back directly."

Annie hurried out of the barn. She dodged around the lumbering wagons that were crowding into the wide dirt yard. Hooves clopped, harnesses jangled, wheels rattled. Already three or four glossy brown mules were dipping their noses thirstily into the water trough.

Annie spotted her mother, anxious and pale, stepping out of the station house to talk to the chief drover of the mule train. Seeing them with their heads together, Annie hung back near the side of the yard, reluctant to break into a grown-up conversation. But the drover looked over at Annie and raised a hand to signal her over. Annie obeyed.

"One of our mules has been having trouble breathing," the drover said to her. "Your mother tells me your father's in a bad way, but you know where things are in the barn. I need some medicine. Is there any belladonna there?"

Annie nodded. "We have a couple bottles in the remedy cabinet. I'll go get one."

She ran lightly to the barn. Entering the tack room, Annie opened the small wooden wall cupboard. The various horse remedies were lined up, same as always. Except—

Annie paused, confused. She made herself study the cupboard carefully again.

"When I opened this cupboard yesterday, I just know there were two full bottles of belladonna, right in front," she muttered.

Today there was only one.

She lifted the remaining bottle. It felt awfully light. She couldn't see through the thick, dark brown glass, so she shook the bottle next to her ear. The faint, hollow splash inside told her that it was almost drained.

With a knot of dread in her throat, Annie walked back outside with the bottle. She handed it to the drover. "I hope that's enough, sir. The bottle's nearly empty."

"Thanks," the drover replied. "A few drops are all it should require. Belladonna's right powerful."

"I know—that's what worries me," Annie said. She turned to her mother. "There was a lot more of that stuff in the cabinet yesterday, I'm just certain. Ma, what if somebody stole it and gave Magpie a big dose?"

Mrs. Dawson drew in a sharp breath. "Would that have made her go loco like she did?"

The drover frowned. "You say a horse of yours was acting loco—and some belladonna's missing? Was she frantic and wheezing and staggering around?"

Annie turned to him excitedly. "Yes—like her insides were on fire."

The drover rubbed his lean, whiskered chin. "That sure sounds like belladonna poisoning." He held up the bottle in his hand. "A little belladonna can cure a horse, but too much can . . . well, it could kill."

Annie clasped her hands together. "How fast can belladonna poisoning take effect? The stagecoach hadn't been here more than a half hour before our horse took sick."

"It depends on how big a dose the horse got," the drover judged. "But it can take effect pretty quick."

Ma gasped. "Who'd do such a thing?"

Annie burst out, "I think I know, Ma. It was that stagecoach guard. I have proof!" Her hand slipped into her pocket, feeling the little tuft of green threads she'd tucked away.

Her mother's face darkened with concern. "Chet Ambrose?"

The drover's eyes widened. "Chester Ambrose?" he repeated.

Ma frowned. "That's right—a stocky fellow, with dark

hair and a big beard. He was working on the stage that came through here last night. Why, do you know him?"

The drover raised an eyebrow. "Don't know about the beard, but otherwise the description fits a feller I knew. He used to work the southern route for the Butterfield line when I did."

Annie's heart leaped. Did he know something about the man she suspected of poisoning Magpie?

The drover scratched his neck and made a disgusted face. "He was a mean-spirited scoundrel, right enough. Last year, after I started working for the Overland Express, we caught him sneaking at night into our camp, just outside of Sacramento. He was trying to cut some of our harness traces."

Annie's mother raised her eyebrows. "Why on earth would he do that?"

"Apparently he took the rivalry between Butterfield and the Overland way too serious," the drover said. "But we got him arrested for that trick in Sacramento. The Butterfield bosses fired him afterward, or so I heard."

"Good for them," Ma declared.

"He was plenty sore," the drover went on. "I still remember him yelling after us as the sheriff led him away in handcuffs, 'I'll make the Overland Express pay for this! You can't ruin Chet Ambrose like this! I'll get my revenge!'"

Annie felt a chill creep up her spine.

She faced the drover with steady eyes and a pounding
heart. "If this Chet Ambrose is the same Chet Ambrose
you knew . . ."

Mrs. Dawson put an arm around Annie's shoulders.
"But if he hates the Overland Express so much, why would
he work for it?"

"He said he wanted revenge," the drover said. "What
better way to get revenge than by working from inside the
company?"

As the drover walked off to treat his sick mule, Ma
took Annie by the arm. "How can you be so sure Ambrose
poisoned Magpie?"

Words bubbled out as Annie told her mother about
the faked arrow wound, the boot print, the snagged
green wool, and the blood-crusted pocketknife. As she
was talking, Davy came running from the barn, waving the
McGuffey's Reader. He proudly showed Ma his sketch of
the boot print as Annie finished telling the story.

Ma sighed unhappily. "Your father did mention to me
this morning that there was a wound on Magpie's flanks—
just before the . . . accident. Oh, I wish he were here to
help sort this out!"

Annie cast a worried look at the station house. "I
know. But I've already sorted it out, Ma. Don't you see?
Ambrose faked the arrow wound so we'd blame Magpie's
poisoning on Indians. He figured it would stir up the
old trouble between the Overland Express and the

Indians. That's his revenge!"

"Now that I think on it," Ma slowly recalled, "Ambrose was awful quick to blame Redbird for meddling with the horse this morning. Shooting off that gun and all, like he wanted to draw attention—"

Just then, the sound of crashing underbrush and pounding footsteps came from the pine scrub. Annie turned toward the noise, muscles tensed.

Billy burst from the trees and leaped across the yard, weaving through the clutter of freight wagons. "Annie, where's Redbird?" he yelled.

"In the station house," Annie called.

"Quick, fetch her out here!" He gasped for breath. "Magpie's getting worse!"

CHAPTER 13
NO TIME TO LOSE

Curious drovers clustered around Billy, and Jeremiah came striding from the barn. Redbird darted out of the station house. "Billy? What's wrong?" Her slender dark face was taut with worry.

Billy fought to catch his breath. "For a while Magpie seemed to be calming down. But then suddenly she started to tremble and sweat, and she was fighting to breathe. She was trying to lie down—I had to keep pulling her back up. I came here quick as I could."

"Sounds like the beginnings of colic," Redbird said, frowning with concern.

Annie felt her stomach tighten like a fist. She knew colic could be deadly. All her excitement about solving the mystery turned sour. What good did it do to know *how* Magpie had been poisoned, if the poison still killed her?

Redbird laid a hand on Mrs. Dawson's shoulder. "If it's

colic, I think I can help her. But you need me here, too, don't you?"

Ma sighed. "You said yourself there ain't much to do now 'cept wait for James to wake. You go on and help that pony. I'll stay by my husband."

Redbird turned and ran back toward the station house. "I'll get my medicine pouch!" she called over her shoulder.

Annie tugged miserably on Billy's elbow. "Well, at least we know what's wrong with her—belladonna poisoning. It seems the stagecoach guard took some from Pa's remedy cabinet and gave her a whopping big dose."

Jeremiah looked startled, and Billy whistled in surprise. "I thought you said he was a company spy," Billy said.

"Well, Pa got it wrong. He ain't a spy, he's just crazy. He did it for revenge on the Overland."

"Then who knows what sort of trouble he's been stirring up along the route?" Jeremiah put in.

Annie clenched her fists. "And just think what he could be up to next. We ought to stop him before he hurts any more horses."

"Or people," Jeremiah added, his voice thick with anger. "If he hadn't messed around with Magpie, your pa wouldn't have got hurt." Annie felt warmed by Jeremiah's loyalty to her father.

"And to think that *he* was going to report *Pa* to the Overland bosses," Annie said, her temper rising. "He said he'd get Pa fired!"

"He still might, when he gets to the end of the line," Ma said. There was a sharp line of worry between her eyebrows.

"*If* he gets to the end of the line," Billy said. "But he won't, not if I have anything to do with it. Annie's right. We've got to stop him!"

Just then, Redbird came running out of the station house. "I've got my pouch. Ready to go with me, Annie?"

Billy caught Annie by the arm. "But I need you to ride the trail east with me, to catch Ambrose!"

Annie stood uncertainly between Billy and Redbird. Her feelings seemed all jumbled inside. The only thing her mind could see was Magpie, staggering in the gully, shuddering with pain.

"You're the fastest rider at the station, Billy," she began in a faltering voice. "Shoot, you're one of the fastest riders in the whole Pony Express. If anyone can catch up to the coach and stop Ambrose, it's you. Why do you need me?"

"Because you're the one who found the proof," Billy insisted. "Nate Slocum won't be inclined to accuse his guard of such a crime. I reckon you can explain things better than I can." He smiled ruefully. "I've kinda got a reputation as a tale-teller, remember? Slocum might disbelieve me."

Ma blew out a sigh. "Billy's right, Annie," she said. "Slocum will need a powerful lot of convincing. Ambrose has been filling his ear with all sorts of bad words about your pa and Red Buttes. He'll believe the two of you better than just one. Besides, you're a good rider—you won't slow Billy down much. The coach can't have gone too far. It's only been a couple of hours."

Tears sprang to Annie's eyes. "But I can't go so far from the station with Pa sick," she protested. "Going down into the scrub is one thing, but riding miles away to the east—"

Mrs. Dawson took her daughter squarely by both shoulders. "I'm here for Pa," she said. "So is Redbird. The best thing you can do for him, Annie, is to clear his name and save his job. Now you saddle up and get going."

Annie made her decision in a split second. "All right." And suddenly, her spirits leaped at the thought of the ride she was about to take.

"Good luck, Annie," Redbird said. "I'll do everything I can for Magpie, I promise. Mrs. Dawson, keep dabbing Mr. Dawson's head with water to hold the swelling down. I'll be back soon!" She turned, plunged into the scrub, and was quickly gone from sight.

Jeremiah clapped Billy on the shoulder. "Stormy's in the barn, ready and rested. You can saddle him up. I'll saddle Surefoot for you, Annie. You're used to riding him, ain't you?" He threw Annie a look that told her he knew exactly what she'd been up to last night.

Annie hesitated. "But what about regulations?" she asked her mother. "I know we ain't supposed to use those horses for personal affairs."

Ma put her hands on her hips. "If this ain't official Pony Express business, what is? My stars, Annie, get a move on!"

&

Annie crouched tightly in Surefoot's saddle, feeling the wind sting her face. Her long pale braids bounced on her back as the horse galloped flat out. As if making up for yesterday's clouds and rain, the sun beat down hard as the trail swung eastward out of the pine scrub. Ahead of her rode Billy, astride the palomino named Stormy.

"I don't know this leg of the trail," Billy shouted above the thunder of hoofbeats. "I always go the other direction, west towards Devil's Gate. Is it flat most of the way?"

"Nearly all the way to the Platte Bridge Station," Annie called back, remembering the few trips she'd taken along this river road. "But there's lots of rocky parts."

To their left, the red buttes thrust up out of the barren plain, miles in the distance. To their right, the rain-swollen North Platte churned furiously. The water foamed white as it rushed over a spill of rocks and a ruined beaver dam.

"They ain't even gone three hours, right?" Billy yelled over his shoulder. "We should catch them before the next relay station."

"Depends on how fast Slocum was driving," Annie answered. "Remember, he was making up for lost time."

An hour later, they galloped into the relay station.
Unlike Red Buttes, which was a home station, this smaller
station was little more than a ramshackle shed, with a
single station hand tending a few ponies. He popped out
of his tiny cabin, surprised to see Billy and Annie galloping
toward him. "We don't need to change horses," Billy
explained, reining in Stormy briefly. "Did the stagecoach
just come through here?"

"About ten minutes ago," the station hand reckoned.
"What's doing?"

"Got to catch 'em—can't explain!" Billy whipped his
black hat off his head and waved good-bye with it. He dug
his heels into Stormy's sides and bolted down the trail.
Annie waved her arm to the baffled station hand and
urged Surefoot after Stormy.

Thundering up a small, rocky rise, Annie spotted the
stagecoach, far in the distance. She pointed it out to Billy
with a triumphant thrust of her arm. "There they are!"

Puzzled, Billy reined Stormy to a halt. "But why are
they stopping? It looks like they're trying to ford the river."

Annie pulled up Surefoot beside him. "That's odd.
Stagecoaches 'most always cross the river at the new toll
bridge, just a little ways east of here."

Billy frowned. "Maybe Ambrose is afraid of being
stopped at the toll bridge," he suggested. "Maybe he talked
Slocum into fording here instead."

Annie studied the scene. Beside them, the North

Platte surged past with a huge, deep rumble. She shook her head. "Generally this stretch of the river is wide and kind of lazy. But with all that rain last night, today it looks almost like flood season. It'd be plumb foolish to cross here today." Her eyes widened. "You don't reckon Slocum's in cahoots with Ambrose, do you?"

"I doubt it," Billy replied. "But I guess we'll find out soon!"

As they charged down the rocky slope, Annie peered ahead to see that the male passengers had all climbed out of the stagecoach. Most of them were putting their shoulders to the back of the coach, preparing to help trundle it across the rushing river.

Then she saw sunlight glint on blond hair a few yards from the coach. It looked like Goldilocks had gone off to one side and was wading across on his own. She felt a stab of misgiving. What was that fellow up to?

From the corner of her eye, she saw Billy dig his heels into Stormy's sides. Stormy flung himself down the slope in a final burst of speed. Surefoot lunged forward too, but he couldn't match Stormy's long-legged gallop. Annie watched Billy draw away from her as he raced toward the stagecoach.

Galloping on, she saw the men clustered around the coach turn around in surprise to watch Billy's headlong approach. Nate Slocum, pulling on the horses' heads, stopped and stood waist-deep in the water.

Annie could pick out Chet Ambrose's broad back in his green coat. He crouched suddenly as Billy neared, as if he hoped to find somewhere to hide midstream. As she watched, he abruptly dropped the wheel rim he'd been holding. The coach lurched dangerously to one side.

Her heart in her throat, Annie urged Surefoot on. A desperate cry reached her ears. It was the woman passenger, screaming from inside the tipping coach. Annie saw the woman's son stick his head out the side window in panic.

Goldilocks whirled around, splashing his way back to the coach. He grabbed the sinking fourth wheel—just in time. Annie felt a surge of relief as the four men passengers, struggling, righted the heavy coach. Annie was close enough now to hear them calling directions to one another.

Then she glimpsed Chet Ambrose, thrashing his way downriver from the coach to deeper waters. Throwing his arms forward, he dove. For a moment, he disappeared under the surface. Then she spied his dark head, glistening wet like an otter, popping up several yards farther on.

CHAPTER 14
BROUGHT TO JUSTICE

Billy turned Stormy's head and rode downstream along the bank, following the swimming Ambrose. Piles of boulders crowded close to the river's edge. Stormy could barely pick his footing along the narrow strip of land. Meanwhile, the swift current was sweeping Chet Ambrose out of sight.

Urging Surefoot along the trail toward the fording stagecoach, Annie clutched anxiously at the saddle horn. It was so hard to watch and not be able to help.

Suddenly she saw Billy reach up and grab a low-hanging branch of a twisted cottonwood tree that grew crazily out of the jumbled rocks. Annie gasped. Hoisting himself out of the saddle, Billy swung over the river in one lithe motion—and dropped into the roiling water.

Annie and Surefoot swerved past the ford and hurried down the riverbank to fetch Stormy. She caught the winded palomino's trailing reins, then turned to scan the river as she fought to catch her own breath.

A hundred yards downstream, in the middle of the boiling current, she spied Chester Ambrose's dark head. One green arm waved wildly in the air.

And then, just upstream, Annie saw Billy swimming hard toward Ambrose.

She heard the stagecoach passengers shouting behind her as they watched the two swimmers. Annie twisted the reins tight in her hands, willing Billy to swim safely. She saw him latch one arm around a boulder a few yards out from the bank. Then he carefully extended his other arm toward the battered guard.

Ambrose, mouth open in terror, clutched at Billy's outstretched hand. His handclasp held for a moment, then broke off. Ambrose's dark head disappeared underwater.

Then Annie saw Billy plunge under, too. She felt an icy jolt of fear. Did Billy dive under—or did some powerful current suck him down?

Despair choked Annie's throat. Someone as brave and cocky and full of life as Billy couldn't die—he just couldn't! Without thinking, she dropped Stormy's reins and slapped Surefoot on the flanks. The little roan sprang forward and began to scramble along the riverbank, hooves striking on the rocks.

Holding tightly to the saddle horn, Annie kept her eyes pinned on the swollen current. The nimble horse brought her closer and closer. A moment later, she saw one head alone bob to the surface.

A dark head.

"No!" Annie cried into Surefoot's reddish mane. "Ambrose should be the one to drown—not Billy!"

Then she spied a second head, pressed against the big man's shoulder. It was Billy, pulling Ambrose to safety!

Surefoot scraped to a halt on the boulder-strewn riverbank. Annie slid out of the saddle before the horse had even stopped. Looking around frantically, she spotted a dead tree limb, probably torn from a nearby trunk by last night's storm. She hoped it was long enough to reach from the shore to the men struggling in the river. She grabbed it with both hands and dragged it to the water's edge.

Now she could see Billy's desperate face midstream, struggling just to stay above the surface. His blue eyes pleaded for help.

Annie stepped onto a flat boulder in the water, dragging the branch after her. She worked the far end of it into the rushing river. The fierce current seized the limb and whirled it into the middle of the river. Annie spun around, fighting to hold on. The rough bark tore at her palms.

Annie stumbled as the current pulled the tree forward. She slipped off the boulder but kept her balance, splashing into ankle-deep water.

The tip of the branch swung near Billy and Ambrose. With a huge effort, Billy heaved up one arm and grabbed the branch. Annie clung on fiercely, but the weight of the two swimmers dragged the bough down, and it began to slip out of her hands.

Then it held fast. "Now *pull*." She heard Nate Slocum's voice behind her. Annie pulled on the branch with all her might. Just behind her, she was aware of Slocum and some of the passengers straining to help her. Together, they hauled in the big limb, hand over hand, like a giant wooden fishing line. They towed Billy and Ambrose to the shallow waters by the bank. The four men passengers waded in to grab Billy and the guard and haul them to shore.

Ambrose looked half-dead. His beard, hair, and clothes streaming wet, he collapsed on the shore and gasped for breath. Billy spluttered and coughed up water. His body began to shake uncontrollably.

The woman passenger hurried up, her skirts soaked from wading out of the stranded coach. In her arms she held a couple of buffalo robes from the stagecoach. "Keep them warm," she insisted. "With the strain and the wet and the cold, they could get pneumonia."

Both survivors were swaddled quickly in the buffalo robes. Nate Slocum took Ambrose by the shoulders. "What possessed you to swim off like that?" he demanded.

Ambrose's eyes grew wild with fear.

"He was just trying to get away—the outlaw," Annie said bitterly.

"Outlaw?" Slocum stiffened. "An employee of the

Overland Express?" His eyes narrowed at Annie.

"I've got proof." Annie dug her hand deep in her pocket. "Do you know this knife, Mr. Slocum?" She pulled out the folding pocketknife.

"Why, yes," Slocum replied. "It belongs to Chet here. Where'd you find it?"

"In our barn." Annie paused. "And remember that pony that went mad last night? This knife was lying just outside her stall, at the back end of the barn. But Mr. Ambrose had no call to be there last night. The coach horses he was unhitching were stabled at the front."

Slocum folded his arms, still looking skeptical. Flipping out the knife blade, Annie pressed on. "The knife's got blood and horse hairs on it—black and white horse hairs. And that pony now has a slash on her flanks."

"She was hit with an Injun arrow that morning!" Ambrose burst out, raising his head. "This fool of a boy told me about it."

Billy forced his teeth to stop chattering long enough to say, "Those Indians didn't shoot arrows at me—I was just telling a tale."

Annie looked up at Nate Slocum's hard blue eyes and thought she saw a glimmer of belief there. Drawing courage, she hurried on to tell him everything she knew— about the missing belladonna, Ambrose's murky past, and the strands of green wool she'd found on the wall of Magpie's stall. "And in a wet spot on the floor, we found this boot print." She held up the McGuffey's Reader, opened to the flyleaf with Davy's inky sketch.

Slocum's brow lowered. "Ambrose, let me see your boot," he demanded. Before the guard could jerk away, Slocum reached under the buffalo robe and trapped his ankle. He pulled out the man's boot and exposed its sole to view.

Everyone crowded around to compare Ambrose's boot to the sketch. The sole was crossed with the same zigzags as Davy had drawn.

Slocum rubbed a hand over his face. "You've betrayed me, Ambrose—me and every other man who rides for the Overland Express."

Ambrose flung his head up defiantly. "I hate the Overland. I hate you all. I'm glad that horse went crazy, and I'm glad she kicked Dawson in the head. I'd do it over again in a minute."

"Hold him, fellas," Slocum instructed the men on either side of Ambrose. As they pinned Ambrose's arms, Slocum took a pair of handcuffs from the guard's belt. "Never thought I'd have to use these on *you*," the driver said as he snapped the cuffs on Ambrose's thick wrists.

Goldilocks tapped Annie's shoulder as Slocum started to lead Ambrose back toward the ford. "Is the poor horse he poisoned all right?"

Annie threw him an anguished look. "I—I don't know yet."

Ambrose, still writhing in Slocum's grip, raised his eyes, cruel as a snake's. "There ain't no cure for a belladonna overdose, you know," he sneered. Annie felt her body go rigid with fury.

Nate Slocum gave Ambrose a warning jerk on the arm. "There is one cure—time," he corrected him. "If that horse lives twenty-four hours after getting the poison, she has a good chance of making it."

Annie swallowed hard. "I've got to get back to Red Buttes, then, and see if she's all right." She hesitated, looking at Billy, still shivering under the buffalo robe. "When do you figure you can ride back, Billy?"

"He shouldn't be riding, after what he's been through," Nate Slocum decided. "He'll need rest, and hot soup. We'll take him with us in the coach to the next home station and see he's fixed up. Do you want to come with us?"

Annie shook her head. "Thank you kindly, but my pa's not out of danger yet—I've got to get back to him. And like I said, the poisoned mare might need some tending to."

"Well, the Overland Express owes you a great debt of thanks," Mr. Slocum said. "I should have known better than to listen to Ambrose's complaints about your pa."

Annie brightened. "Then you won't report him to headquarters after all?"

"Report him? Oh, I'll report him all right," Nate Slocum said gravely. Then she spied a small twinkle in his stern blue eyes. "He'll be reported for being an honest, dutiful stationmaster—and for raising a fine, loyal daughter."

Annie blushed right up to the roots of her pale hair.

"Can you ride back to Red Buttes on your own?" Slocum went on. "A slip of a girl like you?"

Annie drew herself up tall. "I made it here, didn't I? And I kept up with the fastest rider in the whole Pony Express. Getting home should be easy as pie, Mr. Slocum."

❧

The firelight flickered that night on the walls of the station house. Annie sat curled in the chair by the hearth, a book spread open on her knees. Her head kept falling forward on her chest as she drowsed off.

"Annie!" Davy called in a warning voice.

Annie's head jerked up.

"You did it again. You fell asleep." Davy threw her a warning look. "You promised me you'd stay awake to keep me company. I don't want to go to sleep yet . . . not in there." He gestured uneasily toward the sleeping quarters where their father still lay.

"I'm sorry, Davy. I'm just so worn out."

"It ain't every day you ride at breakneck speed to Platte Bridge and back," Mrs. Dawson said gently from the doorway. "It's no surprise you're tired, Annie."

Annie jumped to her feet. "You look tired, too, Ma,"

she said. "Watching over a sickbed is a worrisome job. Let me take your place for a while. You rest and get something to eat."

"I believe I will, Annie," Ma said. She reached back to tuck a few loose strands of hair into the knot on her neck. "I could use a bowl of that good stew Davy warmed up for us."

Davy smiled, his face flushed with pride.

Annie slipped into the dimly lit bedroom. She took a wet cloth from the tin basin beside the big bed and gently bathed her father's temples. Then she settled into the rocking chair near his pillow. Her father's face looked strange—like a pale, waxy mask.

Rocking, Annie felt herself drift off to sleep again. Her eyelids fluttered. For a confused moment, she imagined seeing her father's eyes open. She started awake and looked over at the man in the bed.

His eyes *were* open!

Joyfully Annie sprang to her father's side. "Ma? Ma! Come here!" she called over her shoulder.

With an anxious step, her mother came to the doorway. She uttered a soft, astonished cry when she saw her husband looking at her.

Pa licked his lips and struggled to sit up. "What time is it—why am I here? Ain't there chores to do?"

"Jeremiah and Annie have done all the chores," Ma said, laying a hand on his cheek. "Magpie kicked you in the skull. You've been unconscious all day. Does your head hurt?"

Pa winced. "Like a house afire. I'm powerful thirsty—"

Annie quickly poured a mug of water for him from the pitcher by his bedside. He took it and sipped thankfully.

"The stagecoach left already?" he went on, confused. "Slocum got off all right?"

"He did," Ma said. "And—well, Annie, why don't you tell him?"

Annie bent over her father. "We found out what affected Magpie, Pa. The stagecoach guard—Ambrose—snuck in and poisoned her with belladonna he stole from our remedy cabinet. He made that cut on her flank, too, to make it look like the Indians had shot her with a poisoned arrow. I reckon he hoped to stir up trouble between the Overland Express and the Indians."

Mr. Dawson looked puzzled. "Do I hear you right? Ambrose was sabotaging the Pony Express?"

Ma leaned forward. "Annie figured it all out after the coach had left. She rode all the way to Platte Bridge to capture him, too."

"With Billy," Annie added. "Billy hauled Ambrose out of the rapids and everything."

Pa smiled weakly. "You'll have to tell me the whole story tomorrow. I can't take it all in now."

Annie clasped her hands. There was one more thing she felt he'd want to know. "But the best part, Pa, is that

Mr. Slocum ain't going to report you after all. In fact, he said he'd praise you to the bosses in St. Joe."

Her father shut his eyes in relief. "You did good, Annie. You and Billy." He took her hand in his big, callused palm and held it gently.

"And Redbird," Annie added loyally.

Ma nodded. "Right from the start, Redbird felt certain that Magpie'd been poisoned. She made sure that pony never had the chance to lie down and let the poison settle."

Pa finished another sip of water. "Sounds like just the right thing. Did it work?"

Annie's heart fell. She and Ma traded worried glances. "Well, we ain't sure yet," Mrs. Dawson admitted. "It looked bad this afternoon, like maybe colic was setting in. Redbird went up the ridge to watch over Magpie. But she's been there a good long while," Ma added hopefully. "I got to figure that's good news. If Magpie can just stay alive long enough for the poison to work out—"

Just then, a thrilling whinny sounded from the yard outside. Annie leaped to her feet. She'd know that whinny anywhere. "Magpie!" she cried.

She ran to the station door and threw it open. There was Redbird, leading Magpie in a circle around the station yard. The mare moved stiffly, still favoring her sore flank. But when she tossed her head, Annie could tell that her old spirit was back.

"She's well, Annie!" Redbird called out gleefully. "The

effects of the poison have finally worn off. She's calm and strong again."

Annie ran out and threw her arms around Magpie's black-and-white neck. The pony rubbed her muzzle against the girl's shoulder with a soft whicker of pleasure.

"You saved her life, Redbird," Annie declared.

Redbird, grinning, shook her head. "I just kept walking her, that's all. You're the one who really saved her life."

1860

A Peek into the Past

LOOKING BACK: 1860

Crowds in Sacramento cheered wildly when the first Pony Express run was completed.

When Johnny Fry, the first Pony Express rider, galloped off from St. Joseph, Missouri, on April 3, 1860, crowds cheered wildly. The Pony Express promised to carry mail from Missouri to California in just ten days—more than twice as fast as any other mail service! No wonder Annie Dawson felt thrilled to be part of such a vital enterprise.

In 1860, half a million people lived west of the Rocky Mountains, many of them brought by the California Gold Rush in 1849. But they were isolated from the eastern half of the country. To reach the West Coast, settlers traveled six months by covered wagon along the Oregon Trail, a rutted track that crossed the lonely prairies and cut through the Rockies. Mail took three weeks to reach California by steamship. John Butterfield's stagecoach company—the one Chet Ambrose once worked for—carried mail along a south-western route, but even the fastest Butterfield coaches took 23 days and nights to rumble from Missouri to California.

A stagecoach on the trail

Then William H. Russell, president of the Central Overland & Pike's Peak Express Company, had a brainstorm: Why not use a relay chain of fast horseback riders to carry the mail west from St. Joseph, Missouri—the place where the East's train tracks and telegraph lines ended? From there, it was 1,840 miles to Sacramento, California, where mail could be loaded onto steamships for delivery to San Francisco. Russell set up 190 Pony Express stations between St. Joe and Sacramento, roughly

The Pony Express route crossed almost 2,000 miles of rugged and dangerous territory.

ten miles apart. Most were relay stations—usually no more than lonely shacks—where riders switched horses. Every 75 miles or so were larger "home" stations where fresh riders waited to carry mail on the next leg. Home stations were often trading posts, forts, or long-established lodgings along the Oregon Trail. Red Buttes was a real Pony Express home station, located beside the North Platte River in the vast Nebraska Territory. (On today's maps, it would be just west of Casper, Wyoming.)

A Pony Express station in Nebraska

Nearly 500 horses were bought for the Pony Express. Long-legged racehorses were used for the prairies, sturdy mustangs like Magpie and Surefoot for the mountains. No expense was spared to obtain the finest horses possible. They carried extra-light western saddles and a specially designed saddle cover, the *mochila*, which could be slung rapidly on and off. It had four mail pouches, one at each corner, fastened with tiny padlocks. The saddle, bridle, and mochila together weighed no more than 13 pounds; the mail itself weighed 15 pounds or so.

And in the saddle was a Pony Express rider, usually weighing less than 125 pounds. The

*The **mochila**, with its cargo of mail, was tossed from rider to rider.*

company hired 80 young men for this job, at excellent
wages of about $25 a week. That was more than a station-
master made. Few of the riders were older
than 20; many were orphans. Dressed in
light, sturdy buckskin clothing, hats pulled
low against dust and sun, they galloped
from one home station to the next, changing
horses five or six times in between. Speed
was so important that riders changed horses
in less than two minutes.

Pony Express riders carried only a knife and a pair
of revolvers for weapons; even a rifle would have added
too much weight. If attacked, riders were instructed to
rely on their speedy horses to escape danger, rather
than stay and fight. This proved a shrewd strategy, for
only one rider ever died during a run. Considering the
wild, deserted territories they rode through, this was
indeed an amazing record.

A fresh horse and rider race away from a Pony Express station after a quick handoff.

Although Annie Dawson is fictional, her friend Billy Cody was a real Pony Express rider. Only 15 years old, he rode the route between Red Buttes and Three Crossings to the west. Cody was famous for his pluck; wagon train passengers recalled

Bill Cody as a young man

him gaily shouting out the news he carried as he thundered past them. He once finished his regular 76-mile run only to find that the next rider had been killed by Indians; he rode another 85-mile leg immediately, then made the return trip, traveling 322 miles nonstop on 21 different horses.

Sending a letter by Pony Express was expensive: $5 per half ounce at first, later reduced to $1. That would equal about $30 today. Customers wrote on thin tissue paper to keep letters as lightweight as possible.

Western newspapers relied on the Pony Express to bring the freshest news from the East. In the months before the Civil War, the Pony Express

Pony Express stamps on the top letter show that it was carried from San Francisco, California, to St. Joe, Missouri.

played a crucial role carrying national news to the West Coast.

Word of Abraham Lincoln's election in October 1860 was sped to San Francisco in just eight days, and the text of his inauguration speech in March 1861 arrived even faster, reassuring California's political leaders and businessmen to stick with the Union. When war broke out in April 1861, the news reached California in only eight days.

A Pony Express rider passes men putting up telegraph poles across the western wilderness. Telegraph lines would quickly put the Pony Express out of business.

Still, the Pony Express did not survive for long. Telegraph lines were finally linked across North America in October 1861, and the Pony Express shut down less than a month later.

Despite its short life—only 18 months—the Pony Express is vividly remembered, thanks to one man: William F. Cody, Annie's friend Billy. After a colorful career as an Indian scout and buffalo hunters' guide, he went into show business as Buffalo Bill Cody, owner and creator of the popular Wild West Show that toured America and Europe in the 1890s. True

to his youthful memories, Buffalo Bill's show included a rip-roaring reenactment of a Pony Express run, with a buckskin-clad rider arriving in a cloud of dust, flinging his mochila swiftly from one trusty mount to the next, then thundering away again. Bill Cody's Wild West Show ensured that the drama of the Pony Express would live on.

ABOUT THE AUTHOR

When Holly Hughes was growing up in Indiana, she loved horses but rarely got to ride. Instead, she devoured mysteries and historical fiction. She also enjoyed taking car trips with her family to different parts of the country. Today, she puts all those interests to work. She writes and edits fiction for young readers, as well as travel guides to places around the world. She lives with her husband, daughter, two sons, and their cat in Manhattan, where she can look out her window and watch horses cantering through Central Park.